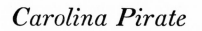

*Carolina Pirate*

## ALSO BY MANLY WADE WELLMAN

*Flag on the Levee*
*Young Squire Morgan*
*Lights Over Skeleton Ridge*
*The Ghost Battalion*
*Ride Rebels!*
*Appomattox Road*
*Third String Center*
*Rifles at Ramsour's Mill*
*Battle for King's Mountain*
*Clash on the Catawba*
*The South Fork Rangers*
*The River Pirates*
*Master of Scare Hollow*
*The Great Riverboat Race*
*Mystery at Bear Paw Gap*
*Specter of Bear Paw Gap*
*Battle at Bear Paw Gap*
*Jamestown Adventure*

# Carolina Pirate

## MANLY WADE WELLMAN

**IVES WASHBURN, INC.**
New York, N.Y.

# CAROLINA PIRATE

Dedication

gratefully

to

Victor S. Bryant

tried friend, true philosopher and master mariner

LIBRARY OF CONGRESS CATALOG CARD NUMBER: 68-25965
MANUFACTURED IN THE UNITED STATES OF AMERICA

# contents

# FOREWORD

I have tried my best to learn all I could about American pirates and the places they went and the things they did in the 1740's. I have travelled on land and sea, I have read books, I have talked to historians and sailors. All these things go into this book.

But the book is fiction. All of the ships are fictitious, and so are all of the people except Governor Gabriel Johnston of North Carolina.

There is even a little fiction mixed into the geography. Nowhere along the Outer Banks of North Carolina is there any such channel as Stryker's Inlet, by name or by nature. But if there had been, maybe adventures as these might have happened there.

Manly Wade Wellman
Chapel Hill, North Carolina

# *peril comes aboard* ⚓ **1** ⚓

Ranald Blaikie squared his shoulders in his new blue coat. He set his feet apart on the quarter deck and grinned up through the rigging at the early morning sky that was bluer than the mist-fluffed sea. He felt the schooner's motion beneath him, he sensed her life and strength. And, for the hundredth time, he told himself that he was her skipper, for the time being at least.

This was how it felt to be skipper of the schooner *Tuscarora,* even if your skippership would last only until you'd put the *Tuscarora* northward tomorrow up Pamlico Sound, and so into the Chowan River to the wharf at Edenton. At nineteen, every day was an important day, and this was an important day indeed.

At Edenton, Captain Mandeville, business partner of Ranald's father, would come aboard and take command. But nineteen-year old Ranald would have had his day of

1

mastership at sea. This was almost like being at sea, though it was Pamlico Sound, with North Carolina's mainland miles to westward and the great succession of the sandy Outer Banks miles to eastward. Even if that soft mist were gone, Ranald would not be able to see land in either direction.

He felt certain that his sinewy figure and freckled face were made impressive by his snug-waisted blue coat and knee-breeches, with their gilt buttons that made them almost a uniform, and by the set of his fine cocked hat. He gazed with what he hoped was a stern and authoritative eye at the seaman at the tiller, then forward to where the *Tuscarora's* bow swivel gun stood in its canvas jacket. No better trading schooner claimed a North Carolina home port this spring of 1741. Even when Captain Mandeville came aboard with cargo and additional men to augment this skeleton crew of six, Ranald would be mate on the *Tuscarora's* voyage to England—a ship's officer, and a good one.

He had to smile in self-congratulation. He glanced to the break of the quarterdeck, where steps led down to the big cabin and his own quarters in the small one. Just now, Captain Mandeville's daughter Enid would be waking up in that big cabin. Her dark maid had carried a breakfast tray down only moments ago. Perhaps Enid would soon come on deck, look admiringly at Ranald's blue coat, and speak of how pleasant it had been to visit the Blaikies at Bath.

"Boat ho!" came the cry of the lookout in the main crosstrees, and Ranald glanced up to see him point with outstretched arm. "Nay, 'tis two boats, yonder off the starboard quarter."

The mist had begun to dissolve as the sun rose to eastward. Ranald could see the boats, like black bean pods, far away among gentle waves. Even at that distance, he could tell that the occupants were rowing frantically. A white cloth flew above the larger boat. Someone waved it back and forth, like a signal.

"Come about to starboard, and quick's the word!" shouted Ranald at once. "Make way close to them, and head into the wind to lay to and see what they are."

The half-dozen men jumped to his orders. The helmsman brought the tiller over while the others shifted sail. Neatly, gracefully, the *Tuscarora* made a great sweeping turn and reversed herself to head southward. The maneuver brought her close to the boats. The white cloth waved more vigorously.

"Now," Ranald called out as they slanted into the breeze from the south, "steady as she is. Hold her for them to come to us."

The *Tuscarora's* reversal of course had brought her considerably to eastward, lessening the distance to the boats. Ranald identified them as a stout longboat and a smaller craft, a dinghy with two pairs of oars. Both seemed to be full of men. The rowers toiled, the boats came nearer and nearer.

"My speaking trumpet," said Ranald over his shoulder, and a chocolate brown youth of Ranald's age hurried to bring it. "Thank you, Cato," said Ranald, and set the trumpet to his lips.

"Ahoy!" he hailed the strangers when he judged them to be within earshot. "Who are you, and what's your plight?"

"Shipwreck!" came the bellowed answer across the waters. "Injured men—sore hurt—"

"We'll help you," called Ranald through the trumpet. "Glad to help sailors in trouble." He looked to his men at the rail. "Stand by to help them aboard," he commanded.

The longboat, propelled by eight oarsmen, distanced its smaller companion and slid close in under the *Tuscarora's* rail. Its crowded company stood up as Cato flung down a rope. A little man in a striped shirt and loose white breeches caught hold and swung aboard, nimble as a monkey. His feet and his tawny head were bare.

"Giles Harrowby's my name, and I thank ye for your help," he said. "Stand by, mates, to help our Captain aboard."

He leaned over the side, and so did Ranald. One man lay at full length in the bottom of the boat, wrapped in a blood-spotted blue cloak. Another man crouched beside him.

"Gently now, mates!" cautioned Giles Harrowby. "How may we fetch him up, Dr. Pilbeam?"

The crouching man turned his red, spectacled face upward. He wore a decent black coat and a ruffled shirt, and his gray hair was clubbed and tied behind. "Steady the boat, all," he said. "Make her fast, fore and aft."

Lines were flung up and lashed to the railing of the *Tuscarora*.

"Now," said the doctor, "we'll lift him, and do you above take him from us."

Ranald and Cato leaned on either side of Giles Harrowby. From below, several stood in the boat to hoist the cloak-wrapped figure as high as they could. Ranald bent to get an arm under the injured man's shoulders. Cato and Harrowby also took hold. Ranald heard a soft moan as they fetched their burden aboard.

"Lay him on the deck," came the voice of the doctor from below, "and give me a hand up that I may tend him."

A powerful shove from below, Cato's ready hand above, and the doctor came over the rail and again squatted beside the injured man.

"Fetch water for him," said Ranald to Cato. "Now, lads, aboard with the others."

They were already swarming over the rail. Farther astern, two more of Ranald's crew helped the smaller boat to tie up and aided its occupants to climb to the deck.

Ranald stooped to watch as the doctor drew aside the blue cloak and revealed a square, pale face, with dark eyes that fluttered open.

"All's well, Captain Haws," the doctor said. "We're aboard a good ship, and you must save your strength while we attend you." He looked up at Ranald. "I am Dr. Rufus Pilbeam. And you—"

"Ranald Blaikie, sir, just now master of this schooner, the *Tuscarora*."

"Whither bound?" asked Giles Harrowby's voice behind Ranald.

"We put out from Bath with the early morning tide," said Ranald, "and we're for Edenton to take on cargo and crew for a voyage to England. Here comes Cato. Give the water to the doctor, Cato."

Dr. Pilbeam took the pannikin from Cato's hand, wet a cloth in it, and carefully bathed Captain Haws' face.

"How is it you're adrift and your captain hurt?" Ranald asked the doctor.

"A Spanish ship hit us below the water line and we got away through a narrow strait, but we went down," replied the doctor.

"A Spanish ship!" repeated Ranald.

He had heard of Spanish raids on coastal towns for months past, ever since England had gone to war over Jenkins' Ear with Spain two years before, but he had seen no victims of such affairs at close hand. "What was your ship," he asked, "and what did you lose with her?"

"Stint your talk," grated Harrowby, now close behind him. "Our ship was the *Surprise*, and sad we were to have her sink from under us, but now we think we may have a craft almost as good as she."

Ranald turned. Giles Harrowby grinned. In his hand was a big brass pistol, and he poked its muzzle under Ranald's nose.

"Easy all, you're our prisoners," Harrowby warned. "And your ship's taken. Look about you and see."

Ranald stared. The men he had rescued swarmed around the outnumbered handful of the *Tuscarora's* sailors, pointing pistols and muskets.

"A foolish move will be your last," Harrowby told Ranald. "We'd hate to kill you, lad. But we take your ship because we need it."

"What piracy is this, you ungrateful dog?" Ranald roared, glaring fiercely at the pistol, but Harrowby only grinned the wider.

"Piracy it is, in sooth," he admitted. "Ungrateful, too, but we're desperate men trying to save our lives—gentlemen sea rovers, young man. Our ship went down from the Spanish shot in her, and we must have another to get away from these waters where pirates have so few friends nowadays."

A solid, dark-bearded fellow with a red scarf on his head had leaped to the quarterdeck above the cabin and had taken the tiller. The halyards creaked above them. Ranald still glared, so surprised and angry that he had not had time to be frightened.

"Who is navigator?" he heard the wounded man gasp.

"I navigate this ship," Ranald growled.

"Then you're in luck, for we'll spare your life," said Harrowby. "You can sail us out of these land-locked waters and on our way beyond, for Captain Haws can scarce speak or move, let alone take bearings and lay courses."

Ranald laughed suddenly, a cold, mocking laugh.

"Nay," Harrowby said. " 'Tis you who are in dire trouble to be laughing."

"Nay," Ranald flung back. " 'Tis you who are in dire trouble if I help you not."

"How, help us not?" blustered another big pirate, tramping close with a cutlass in his hairy hand. "You'll help us or die."

"Aye, help you or die," repeated Ranald, happy to find

that his voice was steady. He was happier that the sound of disputing voices had not reached Enid Mandeville in the cabin. She was a bold girl, too bold some thought. She might hurry into the open to see what the talk was about. And Ranald did not want that, not until he had made good his hoped-for terms.

"Navigate you, sail you to safety," he summed up the demands of the pirates. "That, or die—and if I die, I leave you without navigation. What terms do we make?"

A moment of silence. Then Harrowby pushed the pistol closer.

"You speak boldly, young rooster, but be careful if you speak foolishly, for I will silence you."

That was good advice. Ranald was aware that all the men on deck—the pirates and his own captured mates —listened to him. All the more reason not to speak foolishly, but he was determined to speak boldly.

"True, you will silence me," he said, with an air of concession. "It'll bring me to my end, but it will also end your chance of escape." He looked levelly into Harrowby's set face. "I'll agree to navigate you, upon certain conditions."

"Let him speak," grunted the wounded man at Ranald's feet. "Hear him, if he's reasonable."

"I'll navigate you where you will, if all others of my company may take your long boat and row away, unhurt and unhindered," he said.

"Are you daft?" yelled one of the pirates. "Your men would send pursuit after us."

"Nonsense," Ranald snorted. " 'Tis miles to the nearest shore. Long before they could summon help, I'd have put you to open sea. And that's the word of a gentleman."

"Word of a gentleman," echoed the weak voice of the wounded captain. "Take his word, Harrowby—make the bargain."

Harrowby swallowed.

"Captain Haws gives me my orders," he said. "Your men may go as they will."

"Give them a mast and sail," urged Ranald.

"We'll do no such thing," Harrowby snapped out. "Oars, and a breaker of water—rowing's dry work enough. But that's all."

"Agreed," said Ranald. He looked down at Haws, whose bandaged head was supported by Dr. Pilbeam. "What say you, sir?"

"I say agreed, too," was the response. "I, too, was a gentleman once. Your friends may go."

Ranald looked around. "Hear you that word?" he addressed his comrades. "You're spared, you may row for shore."

Cato had lingered at hand, still holding the pannikin in which he had brought water for Haws.

"I don't go if you stay, Master Ranald," he announced.

"Go you must, Cato, and make report to my father and mother," Ranald told him. "That's my order to you."

"Your father told me I must sail wherever you went," said Cato, softly but stubbornly. "It's his order I'm obeying."

A gnarled, bald little man with one shirt sleeve torn away to bandage his stringy arm glanced shrewdly at Cato.

"Ye mean ye're for joining our rovers' crew?" he asked.

"I stay with Master Ranald," Cato replied, quietly insistent. "He and I were brought up together. He taught me to read and write, he taught me something of navigation as he was learning it . . . "

"Ha, then you may stay," interrupted Harrowby. "Anyone who knows navigation is welcome among us. The rest may go, but this fellow—Cato, is that his name? Well, Cato stays because he asks to stay."

"Into the boat, you others, and off with you," commanded the little man.

"Wait, these aren't the only ones aboard," spoke up Ranald. "Cato, go aft to the cabin and bid Miss Mandeville and her maid come get into the boat. Tell them not to fear, all's safe with them now."

Harrowby exclaimed in surprise, and watched Cato cross the deck, walk down the steps, and knock at the cabin door. It opened, and out came a slender girl in a full-skirted dark dress. After her walked a young woman, her head wrapped in a kerchief, bearing bundles under her arms.

"Enid," Ranald addressed the girl, "I've agreed to stay aboard the *Tuscarora* with these men who've captured her. But you and Miranda will be rowed back to land by the crew. Tell your father how things happened and how I did this to save you and the others."

# sailing with pirates | ⚓2⚓

The whole raffish pirate crew stood and stared, like so many stuffed owls. Ranald faced aft as Enid Mandeville and her maid walked toward him.

"You did well to stay in the cabin till I arranged all things for your safe departure," he said triumphantly. "Go with the boat, and tell my father and mother how I've done the best I could."

"Belay that talk of her going!" cried one pirate, who had just helped hoist a big brass-clamped chest aboard. He stamped across the deck, splay-shouldered and swarthy, grinning to show a gap where his front teeth ought to be.

"Let this sweet lass go?" he blustered. "I vote nay to that, messmates. By her dress she's of a rich family. She could bring us a tidy ransom. And while we wait for the gold pieces to come buy her from us, she'd make this new ship of ours a prettier craft, eh?"

11

"There's something to what Scratch Walker says," spoke up another.

Enid looked at the gap-toothed man with wide, scared eyes, and he laughed aloud.

"What's to be afraid of, missy?" he said. "Ye can see that I've lost my teeth and can't bite you."

He reached out a hand, as though to take hers. Swiftly Ranald shoved him back.

"Touch her," Ranald warned, as fiercely as he could manage, "and you'll have me to kill."

"And if you kill Master Ranald you must kill me, too," seconded Cato.

The fellow glared at Ranald, who glared back.

"Stand back from there, Scratch Walker," said Harrowby in a voice of sharp authority. "No harm to our new navigator."

"Ha, that's practical sense," said Ranald steadily, though he was shaking inside. "Over the side with you, Enid, and you, Miranda."

Already the men of the *Tuscarora's* crew were in the boat. They held up hands to the two women and Ranald lowered Enid, then Miranda, over the side.

"God watch over you, Ranald," Enid said. "I'll tell your father, and mine, too, about what happened."

"Godspeed," said Ranald, as he saw the oars dip, and heard the voice of a rower giving directions.

The gnarled little man came to Ranald's side. "My name's Frank Terrell, and I'm gunner of this crew," he said, putting out his hand. "And you're Ranald Blaikie, eh? Scots, by the sound of the name, and Scots by the shrewdness of your bargaining, too. Well, a happy, profitable voyage to both of us."

Dr. Pilbeam had called two men to help lift the wounded Captain Haws. They carried him to the cabin vacated by Enid and her maid.

"Now your duties as a gentleman rover begin," Harrowby said to Ranald. "Set us a course out through those banks and reefs to open sea, and quick's the word."

Ranald looked quickly at the boat as it pulled away with the people he had managed to set free. Then he studied the morning sun.

"Two points to port," he directed. "That will head us for an inlet south of here, and you'd better pray your Spanish ship isn't prowling thereabout."

He walked aft, up the steps to the deck above the cabin, where the stern gun, the tiller on its pivot, and the binnacle were. "Two points aport," he repeated to the dark-bearded steersman. "Or don't you know what that means?"

"I'm Quartermaster," was the reply. "I handle the helm as well as any man afloat. But what navigation is this? You need charts, readings."

"Not in these waters," said Ranald. "I've sailed them since I was ten. We head for Stryker's Inlet."

The bearded face scowled. "Stryker's Inlet? 'Twas through there we scraped in the dark to get away from the Spaniard, and we sank not an hour's floundering way this side. D'ye mean to hang us up there, to be caught and set in chains?"

"I passed my word to do my best for you," Ranald reminded him. "That's enough, I think."

"No more than enough in these sad times for poor rovers," said the steersman. "Once we were welcome in Spanish ports—Havana, Santiago, Saint Augustine, all of them. But in 1739 the Spaniards cropped Master Jenkins' ear for smuggling, and bade him go show it to King George, and England declared war to avenge him."

Ranald knew the tale of the flippant Spanish defiance to England's king, and he knew, too, neighbor men who had enlisted in the effort to take Saint Augustine in Florida, to fight Spanish invaders in Georgia. He knew about bombardments of seaports in the Carolinas and Spanish America, all of this due to what was called the War of Jenkins' Ear.

The helmsman shifted course as ordered, and overhead the pirates nimbly clapped on more sail. The *Tuscarora* made swift way in the direction Ranald had set. Other pirates had entered the hold, and now they were back on the main deck. Ranald heard one of them report to Harrowby that there was no cargo, only provisions for the voyage to England and a magazine of muskets, pistols and powder.

Some of the muskets had been brought up. Frank Terrell examined them, nodding his head as though in approval. Then Terrell mounted the quarterdeck. In one hand he bore a sheaf of folded papers, in the other a scuffed wooden inkstand with a quill pen stuck in it.

"Ranald Blaikie, ye needs must sign articles to join us," he announced. "Here, I'll read ye the matter and explain it."

"And welcome among us," he said, in so friendly a fashion that Ranald took his hand. Shoup did not offer to shake.

"Now, mate, how long can ye be spared from up here?" Terrell asked. "Cap'n Haws wants ye below in the cabin."

"This course can hold for half an hour and upwards," said Ranald, and followed Terrell down to the deck, then descended more steps to the door of the main cabin.

That cabin was square and low-ceilinged, and finished throughout in dark walnut. Two bunks were there, against the bulkheads on opposite sides of the door, and on one of them lay Captain Haws. The cloak that had covered him was flung upon a chair. Ranald saw that the pirate Captain was heavily bandaged almost everywhere.

A white cloth bound his brows and the top of his head. His ruffled shirt had been half-cut from his body, and more bandages encircled his chest and swathed his right arm from fingertip to shoulder. His left hand, too, was bandaged. Bloodstains flecked and splotched the white bandages. The left leg of his knee breeches had been ripped along the outside, and splints of wood were strapped to the leg from above the knee to the ankle, as though to hold broken bones in place. Dr. Pilbeam bent above the wounded man and held a glass of wine to his lips. Cato stood nearby, with a basin of water in his hand.

Haws sipped the wine. His square face was still drawn with pain, but some color had returned to it. He managed a thin smile.

"Here you are, young man," he greeted Ranald.

"Here as ordered, sir," Ranald said tonelessly.

"Come, you're one of us now," Haws said, trying to speak in a strong voice. "I, for one, am glad you're in our company. The doctor says I'll mend, but for days I must lie here like a fish on a grill. We're lucky to have you to navigate us."

"I navigate you because I needs must, sir," Ranald reminded him. "I passed my word to that to save my friends."

"Yet suffer me to say, you've acted and spoken well," said Haws, smiling again. "Ha, you stare. Have you never seen a wounded man before?"

"Never, sir," Ranald told him.

"These wounds are from flying splinters and scraps of wood," Haws said. "A Spanish shot ripped our bulwarks, and I was gashed and smashed—a broken leg, and wounds from which I've bled enough to float a fishing smack. But tell me, young sir, how came you to qualify yourself as an officer of the sea?"

Standing at attention, Ranald explained as briefly as he could. He was a merchant's son, he said, and had sailed small boats from boyhood. Under Captain Mandeville, his father's partner, he had studied navigation and more advanced seamanship. To another question, he replied that Miss Mandeville was Captain Mandeville's daughter. She had been visiting the Blaikies at Bath, and had sailed with the *Tuscarora* to return to her own home in Edenton.

"You did well by her, youngster," Haws remarked. "I trust you'll like us better as time goes on. Where do you keep your charts and instruments?"

"In the small cabin next to this," said Ranald.

"Be that cabin your quarters and place of work, then. Now, there are articles for you to sign."

"I've already signed them."

Dr. Pilbeam had been wiping his square-lensed spectacles all during this exchange. Now he dipped a cloth in the basin Cato held, and bathed Haws' drawn face. "Rest now, Captain," he said. "You must not become too tired."

Ranald bowed stiffly and went out again, to mount to the quarterdeck. "We shift slightly to southward ere long," he told Shoup at the tiller.

"How fares Captain Haws?" Shoup asked.

"The Doctor says he'll mend as the days pass."

"Ha!" Shoup muttered. "What good's a pirate Captain who can but lie helpless?"

"That's for yourself to answer," said Ranald.

"You and I must have some talks as we sail," said Shoup.

Just then the lookout in the main crosstrees called out that he saw land, far away to port on the horizon. Ranald glanced briefly at the sun, then at the compass in the binnacle, and ordered the course shifted one point to southward.

*open sea* ⚓**3**⚓

The nearer they came to the great sandy bar of Portsmouth Island, the more its scrub of trees looked like dark fluff against the morning sky. Ranald counted the pirates on deck and on lookout in the crosstrees. Eighteen in all. With Captain Haws and Dr. Pilbeam below, that made twenty.

Harrowby mounted to the quarterdeck and peered. "What's the closest way out to sea?" he inquired.

"Ocracoke Inlet above, and Swash Inlet below," said Ranald, "but both are much used by fishermen and coastwise craft. You'll have less company if we sail south by southeast to Stryker's."

"And be luckier, maybe," nodded Harrowby. "Blackbeard ran aground in '18, these twenty-three years ago. And a Virginia sloop of war boarded him and slew him."

"As to that, we all but grounded in Stryker's Inlet last evening," said Shoup from where he held the tiller.

"Belike you came midway of the channel," Ranald suggested. "Deeper water lies at the south of the inlet."

"And this *Tuscarora* draws less than our lost ship," observed Harrowby. "Swift she runs, and close to the wind. Where was she built, Master Blaikie?"

"Baltimore, three years gone, but Captain Mandeville altered her keel and restepped her masts at Edenton," Ranald told him. "Captain Mandeville's a sound shipman."

"And father of a passing fair daughter, eh?" Shoup chuckled.

"His daughter doth not enter this talk," growled Ranald.

"Sink me if you don't speak bold at all times," Shoup said, still grinning. "I look for you to be a famous rover."

"Keep your hand to the tiller and your eye to the compass," Ranald advised him. "With this wind, we'll make Stryker's Inlet by mid-morning."

He drew out his silver watch. It was half-past eight, not much more than an hour since the pirates had come aboard. It seemed a year.

The *Tuscarora's* captors lounged here and there on the main deck, grawing hard biscuits and cutting slices of smoked beef. Cato moved among them with a basket of biscuits and a firkin of meat. Ranald strode down the steps to him.

"Why do you wait on them, Cato?" he demanded. "That's not in our contract."

"I asked for the duty, Master Ranald," said Cato, smiling. "Their Cook was killed by those Spanish shots. If I do the cooking, I reckon I needn't help with the fighting."

Dr. Pilbeam appeared on deck. "Glad I am to see these hungry lads having a decent breakfast," he remarked. "Your man Cato's invaluable, sir."

He sandwiched a slice of beef between two biscuits. Ranald helped himself, too. He was surprised at his own hunger.

Harrowby, the Boatswain, ordered a shift of sails. Ranald watched the men jump smartly to their tasks. Most of them were gay figures, with bright-colored head scarfs and shirts and sashes. "They bear themselves in sailorly fashion," Ranald said to the doctor.

"Aye, they're as able seamen as the ablest."

"You seem able at your own profession, sir," Ranald made bold to say.

"A healer's duty is to heal," was the sober reply. "For my being in this particular company, that's a longer story than I can tell you offhand."

Dr. Pilbeam went down to the cabin again. Terrell approached.

"I've looked at those swivels, fore and aft," he said. "I judge they're sound. But we need two broadsides of six-pounders 'ere we go prize-hunting."

"You've been a Gunner for a long time?" Ranald ventured.

"Since I was younger than you," said Terrell. "I began with Bartholomew Roberts aboard the *Royal Fortune*. We took royal fortunes from prizes, and spent them royally. And he led prayers aboard on Sundays, and allowed no fighting amongst us. I was lucky to be ashore when he was taken by the *Swallow,* and died fighting."

"I have heard talk of Blackbeard," remembered Ranald. "What do you say of him?"

"Teach was his true name," said Terrell. "He took good prizes, and he fought and stood off the King's ship *Scarborough.* But another ship of war undid him, up yonder at Ocracoke Inlet."

"I've heard him called a sea-devil," Ranald said.

"He was all black whiskers and burning eyes," nodded Terrell. "He stuck lighted gun matches into his beard for a fight, to make himself smoke fearsomely as he led a boarding party. His men feared him, every one. Yet Henry Johnson was a better sailor and fighter, for all he had but one hand. I was Johnson's Gunner when we took the *John and Jane.* A hard five-hour fight, but Johnson forbade us to harm the prisoners."

"Strange mercy for a pirate," said Ranald.

"Nay," and Terrell shook his head, "only good practical business. Those we spared told the tale at home, and other ships were readier to yield without fighting us. Cap'n Haws follows the same policy. Cap'n Haws is a finer rover than Blackbeard or Roberts or even Johnson, and so you'll find when he takes command again."

They neared Stryker's Inlet. It was a gap between the islands on either side. Ranald mounted to the quarter-deck.

"I saw another way through, half a mile above," said Shoup.

"That is shallower than Stryker's and needs high tide

for safety," said Ranald. "Lay her in to starboard of the
channel. Closer in, I say. Here, give over to me."

Elbowing Shoup aside, he took the tiller. The *Tuscarora* ran before a good breeze from the west, approaching
the bank piled high with sand. Shoup growled something,
but Ranald ignored him, steering close.

"Deep water here at starboard," Ranald said. "Enough
for a ship of this burden, and no touch of her keel at bottom."

"You'd best know what you're doing," Shoup muttered.

Ranald steered the *Tuscarora* as delicately as though
tracing her course with a pencil. The bank to starboard
made a great jut, crowned with a scrubby tree. Beyond,
the channel widened. The banks to either side slanted
away, to form a harborlike space toward the open sea.

"Take over," Ranald said to Shoup.

"So you did steer honestly," grumbled Shoup, and as he
took the tiller he sheathed the big knife at his hip. "Had
you played false, 'twould have been your last act upon
earth."

Harrowby joined them. He laughed aloud.

"Master Blaikie, you meant your word, and we may
take this as proof," he said. "Cap'n Haws asks you to
come to him as soon as we're through the inlet. Head out
eastward, Tucker Shoup." He raised his voice. "You in
the crosstrees, look away for any sign of another ship."

Ranald descended to the cabin. Dr. Pilbeam was there,
measuring drops of medicine into a small glass. Captain
Haws drank the dose and looked up from his pillow.

"At open sea, are we?" he greeted Ranald. "Now prove your right to be Sailing Master. Know you where Grand Cayman is?"

"I've seen it on maps of the West Indies," said Ranald. "South of Cuba, west of Jamaica."

"If it's on the map, you should navigate us there," said Haws. "Lay your course and issue your orders."

Ranald creased his brow. "To get there, we must pass Cuba, full of Spanish war craft."

Haws drew a pained breath.

"We must go to Grand Cayman," he insisted. "Food and water we have aboard, but not the arms and equipment. Point us east of the Bahamas, and so to the Windward Passage betwixt Spanish Cuba and French Haiti." He drew another difficult breath. "Set that course, and see we steer it."

"Gently, Captain," urged Dr. Pilbeam. "Rest now, you have fever to fight."

Back in his own cabin, Ranald spread maps on the table. At once he saw that laying the course would be relatively simple. They had cleared Stryker's Inlet at approximately 76 degrees and ten minutes west, and only a very few miles below 35 degrees north. As for the Windward Passage, Cuba's easternmost cape was almost exactly at 74 degrees west by 20 degrees north.

He jotted figures on a bit of paper, multiplying and dividing. At 35 degrees north, a degree of longitude figured to approximately forty miles. Ninety miles east, then, would bring them to the 74th meridian west. And fifteen degrees of latitude from here to Cuba meant a thousand miles more, with no land along the way until they reached the southern islands of the Bahamas.

He hurried on deck again. Harrowby met him. "Let's have the log afloat, and readings of our speed," said Ranald.

"We've already hove the log, and we're doing eight knots and better with this wind," replied Harrowby. "What course, matey?"

"Due west ninety miles," replied Ranald, "and then due south." He dragged out his big silver watch. "It's ten now. By midnight or earlier, we shift course. Send someone to me in my cabin ere noon."

And he went below again, to study the maps. His course would put them in among the lower Bahamas, and through the channels that separated British-held islands with names like Samana, Acklin's and Great Inague. Their British flag should protect them there. But below the Bahamas, the passage between Cuba and Haiti looked to be no more than fifty miles across, and surely it was full of Spanish peril.

He thought of the morning's adventures. Though Shoup had feared Ranald might play the pirates false, young Blaikie had not once considered going back on his sworn word. But would he have been justified in running the *Tuscarora* to the bank there in Stryker's Inlet, leaving the outlaw crew and their wounded captain stranded, while he took his chance of escape ashore?

He pondered that at grim length. Then he reflected that when the proposition of joining the pirates had been brought up, he had not really demurred. Instead, he had bargained readily and successfully for the lives of his own crew and Enid's safety.

It was giving his word that had bound him, more than any fear of death. Enid and the others must have gotten to safety by now, and would tell the news of the surprise and capture. Meanwhile, Ranald was sailing the *Tuscarora* far out to sea, on lawless errands. The wrongs and the rights of the matter would have to reveal themselves to him later.

A quarter of an hour before twelve a voice summoned him, and he mounted to the open air with sextant and compass. At noon exactly he took the position of the sun, checked direction and time, and reckoned their position. The pirates had clapped on all possible canvas, and the *Tuscarora* was doing nine knots and better. Ranald listened to the seamen singing at their work. He caught some of the words:

"The people they will flock when I hang, when I hang,
The people they will flock when I hang,
The people they will flock unto Execution Dock,
And watch me stand the shock when I hang . . ."

"That ballad was written when Cap'n William Kidd was tried and condemned," Terrell said at his shoulder. "How d'ye like it?"

"The tune's merrier than the words," Ranald ventured. "All I know of Captain Kidd is the tale of his buried treasure."

"And a tale is all it is," Terrell returned. "Blackbeard hid gold somewhere, but never Kidd."

The *Tuscarora* ran beautifully, and Ranald went below, where Cato met him with a noon dinner of stewed beef and turnips.

That afternoon he watched while Shoup turned the tiller over to Scratch Walker and explored the *Tuscarora's* slop chest. Except for Haws, none of the company had clothes save those they had come aboard in. Thankfully they received breeches, shirts, belts and caps. But one or two complained that these clothes were of sober cut and color, and when they heard that they were sailing for Grand Cayman they loudly swore to buy better piratical gear there.

By sundown they had accomplished a good eight hours of steady sailing beyond Stryker's Inlet. Ranald, bringing out his sextant, took the positions of two early stars and reckoned that they had sailed at least seventy miles. Up from the big cabin came an order from Haws that no lights show above decks except for the binnacle, and that Ranald visit him.

Dr. Pilbeam was at Haws' bedside, feeding him broth with a pewter spoon. "How fares it with you, sir?" asked Ranald.

"Poorly, I fear," was Haws' feeble reply. "Yet thanks for your question, which sounds concerned and friendly."

Ranald had spoken in friendly fashion, without thinking. "You sent for me," he reminded him.

"So I did." Haws took more broth. "Tell me the course you laid."

Ranald did so, and Haws made a slight nodding motion, as though in approval.

"Once headed south, we can steer by compass," said he. "You did well, Master Blaikie."

" 'Twas simple navigation," said Ranald. "But I remind you again, the passage between Cuba and Haiti is narrow and perilous."

"I know, I know, but needs must," Haws answered. "Once past that narrow place, we can drive on to the east of Jamaica, and so southward into seas where Spaniards dare not challenge English warships. Then west again, to our landfall on Grand Cayman. How far a voyage do you compute it?"

"A thousand miles to the Windward Passage, at the very least," said Ranald. "From there I have not laid a course, but I should guess it at six hundred or more miles beyond." He pondered a moment. "Below Jamaica, as the map says, are dangerous shallow waters."

"The Pedro Shoals, they're called," Haws informed him. "But if they imperil us, they'll be sorer peril to Spaniards. I know those shoals, but I've navigated worse, and have come off safe and free. You say you know Grand Cayman only from the charts."

"I've heard it called an unlucky landfall for honest sailors," said Ranald frankly, and Haws managed to smile.

"We're not honest sailors, you'll have in mind," he said. "We're pirates, and for us it's a fine haven. Once there we can ship guns aboard, and powder and shot for them, and stout fellows to serve them so we may dare the seas again."

His brief cheerfulness seemed to ooze out of him, and he sank back on the pillow.

"Captain, you must rest," Dr. Pilbeam declared authoritatively. "Bid us good night, Master Blaikie."

Ranald bowed and returned to his own quarters.

# rogues on grand cayman ⚓4⚓

After that, they sailed the *Tuscarora* as Ranald decided and ordered, and it was a swift, safe voyage, two weeks of it.

Before midnight of that first day at sea, Ranald took an observation of the stars that showed them at the 74th meridian, or near enough for practical purposes. He said as much to Harrowby, who sent men aloft to shift sail. Walker at the tiller strove and dug in his hard bare feet to change the course. Around came the *Tuscarora*, until the North Star showed a steady radiance in the night sky above her sternpost. Half a moon was up, enough to catch and kindle the wake she left, a gleaming, dancing line on the water that seemed to lead back to the North Star. Ranald slept in his cabin as they went southward.

He was up next morning at early sunrise. Instead of the fine blue coat and cocked hat he put on the clothes of an ordinary sailor, loose breeches and an open-collared linen shirt. He slung a dirk in his belt and pulled light shoes upon his bare feet. He tied a blue scarf over his hair, with the queue dangling down behind. Up on deck, he found Cato with a mug of coffee in his outstretched hand. Harrowby and Terrell also came to greet him.

"Now you're dressed more like a pirate," said Terrell. "By log and line, we've sailed fifty miles and more from where we changed course. What orders now, Master Blaikie?"

"We keep our present course," replied Ranald, drinking the hot coffee. "How fares Captain Haws?"

"Wretchedly, I fear," replied Harrowby. "Dr. Pilbeam says he tossed and babbled all night, with a burning fever."

"Ha, and is it so?" asked Shoup, coming toward them. "Will he die, think you? Who'll stand for our Captain when he's gone?"

"He's not gone yet," returned Terrell gruffly. "Only weak and sick."

And weak and sick was the report from the big cabin for several days. During that time, they kept to the open sea along the 74th degree of longitude. Several ships came near enough to speak them, British and American vessels inquiring what name they bore and where they were bound. Each query was answered by Shoup or Harrowby, climbing the rail and bawling through a trumpet that they were the *Tuscarora* out of Bath in Carolina, with cargo for the Bahamas.

" 'Ware a Spanish raider in these waters," came back a megaphoned warning from one ship. "*Compeador* she's named, captained by a proud hidalgo, Don Carlos Montero! Full forty guns on decks above and below, and hungry for poor British and American merchantmen!"

"That's the very ship that sank us," commented Harrowby, swinging down from his perch on the rail. "Gobbling every prey in sight."

"As we could gobble that prey yonder," mourned Shoup, gazing after the departing ship that had warned them. "Had we any guns but these swivels, we could take her like a plump partridge."

Every pirate aboard spoke cheerfully to Ranald, with respectful praise for his skill at sailing. They stared as he employed his sextant to observe the sun by day and the stars by night. None knew that this was to gain practice at his assignment as navigator on this perilous journey. He felt assured only by his reckoning by the sun at noon. Cato was his one confidant, and came often to Ranald's cabin to help study the charts.

Cato won commendation, too, for the food he cooked and served. The pirates especially liked the boiled puddings Cato made of meal, sugar and dried currants.

On the sixth morning, gloom seemed to trickle like dark water from the big cabin, where Haws twitched and raved in fevered delirium. But by sundown Dr. Pilbeam emerged on deck to say that a profuse sweat had come upon the wounded man, bringing down his temperature and restoring him to his senses. Ranald, like many another youngster studying for command at sea, had read some works on medicine, and listened to all the doctor said.

"Would not Captain Haws be helped by bleeding?"

Ranald asked, and Dr. Pilbeam frowned as he polished his spectacles.

"Aye, the medical faculty prescribes bleeding, but I dare wonder if 'tis always a good thing," he said. "Oft I have asked myself, doth not the blood mean life and health, and must not a sick man have need of all the blood nature hath given him? I did not bleed Captain Haws but sought to cool him with sponging and medicining."

Ranald forebore to argue with so learned a man, but wondered if this did not go contrary to medical usage.

"I thank heaven that all others aboard with us are well," went on Dr. Pilbeam. "When we come to a port, I trust we can bring green stuff aboard—fruit and vegetables. It fends off scurvy, fresh food like that."

That night, Ranald answered a call to visit Haws. The pirate captain looked pale and thin, but he spoke steadily and sensibly.

"I've stood a grim siege, but now Dr. Pilbeam bids me feel sure of recovery," he said. "I feel stabs and aches in every part of my body, which he ascribes to natural healing. Meanwhile, as I am told, we've made good speed in bright weather, with favoring winds."

"Seven hundred and fifty miles on our way to the Bahamas, as I compute," said Ranald. "By tomorrow night or the next day, we must begin to wend our way among the islands."

"You will have the counsel of Harrowby and Terrell," Haws reminded. "Time and again they have sailed and steered in those waters."

"And Shoup's counsel, too," added Dr. Pilbeam from beside the bed.

"Aye, his counsel with others," agreed Haws, as though in afterthought. "Where do we first approach near to land?"

"Near Samana Island, as I judge by the charts," Ranald made answer. "We should pass near to the east of there, and then southward past Acklin's Island, and so near Great Inague. From there 'tis some sixty or seventy miles to the eastern cape of Cuba."

"Bear away before you come there," warned Haws earnestly. "Lay your course close in to the shore of Haiti. No Spanish ship will hunt us in French waters."

Thus cautioned, Ranald studied his charts even more closely as they sailed the 74th meridian, like a cat footing its way along the top of a fence. They crossed the 24th parallel of longitude, and Ranald stifled a sigh of relief when, as they came in distant view of Samana, Shoup and Harrowby took over the steering without asking him for observations.

"Nay, we've run these little straits so often we could do them blindfold," said Harrowby. "A hundred and fifty miles or so, in and out, to slide in close at the west of Haiti, away from Spanish perils like that *Compeador.*"

A day and a night more of sailing, with shores in view again and again, and now and then a distant ship, until they passed Great Inague and stole southward near a low island that Harrowby called Tortugas. Clouds boiled up next morning and rain fell, but the pirates were cheerful as drops splashed on the deck.

"All the less chance that yonder Spanish swabs will be at us with their long guns and long pikes," commented Terrell as they went on down into the passage.

By dull dawn of their twelfth day at sea, Harrowby called for a shift of course to southeastward. Under brightening skies they moved close to the eastern extension of British-governed Jamaica, dropping the lead frequently to be sure of a safe channel among the rocky huddle of Morant Keys. As they set the prow due west between Jamaica's southern shore and Pedro Shoals, a heavy-armed sloop of war hailed them.

Craftily Harrowby yelled through his speaking trumpet that they had sick men aboard, seemingly infected with a contagious fever. The sloop put about and drew away hastily.

Ranald was at his charts and instruments again, laying their course northwest. Late on the afternoon of their fourteenth day at sea, the lookout in the main crosstrees raised an exultant howl of "Land ho!"

Instantly Terrell sprang into the shrouds and went up the ratlines like a monkey to where the lookout perched. He came tumbling down, with a crinkled grin of relief.

"Grand Cayman, mates," he reported.

Grand Cayman, repeated Ranald in his mind. That was the remote island where British law and control were only sketchy formalities. In went the *Tuscarora*, tacking against a breeze from the west, until Ranald could see a long white shore, clotted here and there with great clumpy belts of dark trees. Houses stood on an open stretch of seaside, and docks ran out. Three ships rode at anchor. As the *Tuscarora* approached still closer, Ranald made out sandy banks spaced here and there between the houses and the line of docks, and a scatter of black dots that must be men on the beach.

The news was carried to the cabin where Haws still lay ill and well-nigh helpless. He sent back orders to anchor well out from the shore and send a boat to see how matters went on Grand Cayman. The boat was lowered, and half a dozen pirates manned the oars, with Harrowby in command.

Ranald watched the boat pull smartly toward land. He noticed the sand banks at closer range now. They seemed to be solidly heaped up against massive palisades of timbers, and here and there were notch-like openings. Through these stared the muzzles of cannon.

"Yonder's Orlop's Rest," Terrell said, pointing out the largest of the string of low brown houses. "Orlop Colton left sea-roving thirty years agone, and built his store and supply house while many fished here for turtles. The turtles have had the sense to swim away from their catchers, but Orlop is still here. He makes many a good gold piece by trade with our sort."

The building was long, with a porch in front. Even at that distance, it looked old and soggy and roughly built. Ranald watched the boat gain a dock. Its occupants sprang ashore and tied up. Several of the men on land joined them. At Orlop's door they met still others, and seemed to enter discussion.

"Is this Orlop Colton rich?" asked Ranald. "What pleasure doth he have, in a place like this?"

"Mostly the counting of those same gold pieces," said Terrell. "And ever is he grasping for more. He'll charge us top prices for any refittings and armings, and you can lay to that."

The sun was going down behind Grand Cayman. Two pirates brought lighted lanterns to hang at the rail and before the steps to the cabin. Other shore lights showed yellow at the windows of the houses. At last the boat returned. Ranald saw a tall, bony old man in shabby finery swing nimbly aboard with the others. The lantern light revealed that the gold lace on his hat was tarnished, and that his braided queue of hair was sparse and gray. As Ranald went below to his own cabin, this stranger and Harrowby also descended. They left the door of the big cabin ajar, and Ranald heard the old fellow greet Captain Haws in a high, squeaky voice.

"Good it doth my old eyes to see you, Reuben Haws," he said, "and what's this I hear of you lying ill? Nay, you look a rosy picture of health."

"Stint your joking, Orlop, I know full well how I look," returned Haws. "Now, what's your string of charges? Give it to me, Harrowby. Zounds, this is barefaced robbery."

"Goods are hard to come by, you'll reflect," said Orlop Colton, with a snicker. "You say you want good seasoned timber to make your new craft a fighting ship, and eight six-pounder guns to arm your broadsides—"

"I left three guns with you two years back for safe-keeping," Haws interrupted. "Yet here are eight written out, with charges against each of them."

"I but ask a fair fee for storage," Colton explained.

"Sure, I'm due something for my good care of them. Five more you'll want, and they're in my magazine, worth every stiver I ask."

"Terrell will look at them tomorrow," said Haws. "Now, a word in time. My men have but the clothes they stand in, and what money they were able to save in their pockets. Sell them new shirts and breeches, I pray you, ere you take their last penny for your filthy rum."

"Sink me without a bubble if my rum's not good New England rum, clean and clear as spring water," Colton protested shrilly. "As fit for gentlemen to drink, I'll warrant you, as the bottle of wine on the table yonder, and that looks to be of the best."

"Pour him a stoup, Harrowby, and one for yourself," directed Haws. "Drink while I study this exhorbitant bill of costs."

Cato fetched Ranald a supper tray. Ranald ate and listened to the talk in the big cabin. There was chaffering over prices for gunpowder, cannon shot and two score other matters. Never had Ranald heard tobacco merchants or ships' chandlers bargain more stubbornly. Orlop Colton argued that he was at great expense gathering wares for sale. Haws told how he had survived the sinking of his ship with but limited resources. At last Colton departed, with many assurances of friendship and good will, and a promise to talk to Haws' representatives on the morrow. A moment later, Harrowby looked in at Ranald's door.

"Captain Haws' compliments, and he desires a word with you," he said.

When Ranald entered the big cabin, he saw Haws on

the bed, pale and drawn-looking in the lamplight. The bargaining session must have drained Haws of what little strength he had. Cato held a bowl, from which Haws slowly dipped a spoonful of soup with his bandaged left hand. He managed a smile at Ranald.

"They tell me you did good service, navigating us hither," he said.

"My promise was to do so," Ranald made cool reply.

"We'll bide here a few days, fitting out for a voyage," Haws went on. "Between the spells of work, the men have leave to go ashore and divert themselves. I trust you, Master Blaikie, and you may shore leave with the rest."

"All thanks for this trust in me, Captain," said Ranald, keeping his tone formally respectful. "But I do no more than I've engaged myself to do, and no less."

Slowly Haws lifted another spoonful to his mouth.

"'Tis plain you don't want to be friends," he said. "Yet I won't answer you in an unfriendly way. Hearkening to you, I remember mine own youth. I had a heart of fire then, and eke a grand sense of honor."

"Then, sir, I wonder that you became a pirate," Ranald felt he must say.

Harrowby muttered dangerously from the doorway, but Haws only smiled again.

"I came to be a pirate for the same reason you did," he said. "It was a case of needs must. In sooth, we all do what we needs must do, or we perish."

"Aye," said Harrowby under his breath, and Haws shifted his head on the pillow to look toward the door.

"Giles Harrowby," he said, "set double watches on deck this night, and again tomorrow. Men under arms, and challenges for all who try to come aboard."

Harrowby knuckled his forehead and turned to mount the stairs.

"Captain, you seem cautious here in anchorage," Ranald said. "I had thought, from the talk I heard, that you and your company were amongst friends here."

"Friends?" Haws said after him. "Nay, Master Blaikie, we're among rogues on Grand Cayman. If we're rogues, too, the more need to guard well against trouble. Honor amongst thieves is no more than a saying, and a false saying at that."

He sank back and waved the bowl away. "Good night," he said.

Cato and Ranald went out together. As they crossed the threshold they glanced at each other, but said nothing.

In his own quarters, Ranald undressed and lay down on his berth. Through the open port came a sound of distant laughter. Some of the pirates must have gone ashore. Probably they were sampling Orlop Colton's grog. Ranald thought that he had successfully navigated the *Tuscarora* many days through strange seas, from North Carolina past enemy coasts to this den of rogues. Given the chance, could he navigate her back again?

He fell asleep without answering himself.

# *refitting and recruiting* | ⚓5⚓

Ranald woke in the faint gray of dawn to a touch on his shoulder and Terrell's seamed face and bald head stooping above him.

"I want ye to come ashore with me, young Ranald Blaikie," said Terrell. "We'll take breakfast in Orlop Colton's taproom, and bargain for guns and powder. Will ye please dress in your fine clothes, that coat and hat and the buckled shoes that make ye look like an officer of the sea?"

"If you say so," agreed Ranald, sitting up.

"And I see a sword hanging yonder on your bulkhead," went on Terrell. "Gird that on. I've my good reasons, youngster, for letting Orlop see we've a true Sailing Master who could take us out of here on the moment, as fast as he fetched us in."

As Ranald made haste to put on his clothes, he saw

that Terrell himself was tricked out in the most impressive gear possible. He wore a red shirt, perhaps borrowed from a shipmate, and the waist of his broad-legged white breeches was bound with a gay sash, streaked in all colors of the rainbow. Into the sash were stuck two big brass pistols. A baldric slung from shoulder to hip bore a sheathed cutlass. In Terrell's ears gleamed two great gold rings. He helped Ranald into his blue coat, then held out two more pistols.

"They're ready loaded and primed," he said. "Put them in your side pockets, but let the handles show."

From inside his shirt Terrell fished a crimson scarf and bound it upon his bald head. Then he led the way out and upward to the deck. There in the dawn stood stocky, bearded Tucker Shoup, also brightly tricked out in striped shirt, blue silk head scarf and a sash holding cutlass and pistols.

"Ready for shore adventure, mates?" Shoup inquired. "The longboat's already lowered."

Down they swung. Four other pirates took the oars and rowed them away to the nearest dock, where they scrambled up to make the boat fast.

Close at hand were those banks of sand-covered logs, with big guns in canvas jackets at notched embrasures. Half a dozen men lounged there, as though on guard, and others sat in groups not far away. Behind the ramparts the row of houses fronted a lane of packed sand, like a very rough street. Logs and old timbers made up the fronts of the buildings. The roofs were of thatch or of coarsely split shingles.

As Ranald and his companions walked toward the big house of Orlop Colton, many stared from the doorsteps. There were both men and women, slovenly clad and curious-eyed. Ranald estimated that the inhabitants of Grand Cayman might number more than two hundred.

Orlop Colton's spry old figure appeared at his door to greet them. By the morning light his face showed as a bunchy mass of fine wrinkles, set with bright black eyes and a long, thin nose like a chisel.

"Good morning, gentlemen all," he hailed them. "I can guess your wish for breakfast—eggs and rashers of bacon, lots of 'em, and rum to wash 'em down."

"Aye, rum," said Shoup eagerly, but Terrell shook his head.

"Coffee, black as the inside of a chimney," he ordered, "until we've done talking business."

"Come in, come in," Orlop Colton urged them.

They followed him through the great open doorway. Ranald found himself in a huge room, slab-walled and beam-ceilinged, with a floor of broad, uneven planks. At one end stood a rough wooden bar, where several roughly dressed men were being served by a broad-shouldered Negro in gay shirt and scarf. Trestle tables were ranged along the other walls, and on them were heaped every imaginable thing a voyage might need. Other articles crowded the shelves above the tables. Colton led them to a smaller table near the bar and waved them toward stools, but paused and squinted up at Ranald.

"And this tall young gentleman?" he prompted.

"Sailing Master Ranald Blaikie," Terrell introduced them, and Colton took Ranald's hand in his hard, skinny fingers.

"He looks as if he rose in rank early," Colton hazarded, showing yellow fangs in a grin.

"He navigated us safely through Spanish waters, all the way from the Carolinas," said Terrell. "Noah himself couldn't have laid a better course for the ark."

They sat, and Colton clapped his hands. From an inner door came an aproned black servant, with a great tray of smoking dishes. Colton himself poured coffee from a sooty tin pot into earthenware mugs for Terrell and Ranald, and filled noggins of rum from a brown bottle for himself and Shoup. They all ate and drank and talked.

Colton had news to tell, of the death earlier that year of one Captain James Flint. Ranald had never heard the name, but Terrell and Shoup pricked up their ears and asked eager questions.

"Died of rum, did Flint," said Colton. "He always drank too much, didn't show sense with his drink like me and Tucker Shoup here. Raving in bed at the last, they tell me, in the rear chamber of a dockside tavern, with only Billy Bones and poor, silly Ben Gunn to tend him."

"Flint hid treasure somewhere," elaborated Terrell. "As much, they say, as Blackbeard's self—took six men ashore on an island to dig the hole, then killed all six in case they might think of sneaking back to dig it up. Some of his other hands might have took that hard, but not a man of them dared question him."

"Are any of Flint's crew here on Grand Cayman, Orlop?" inquired Shoup. "We lost good men when that Spanish dog sunk us, we're barely a score now. We'd like to ship at least that many new mates, of the true roving sort."

"None of Flint's men are here," replied Colton. "They're mostly finding their way back to England, I hear tell. But I can look you out men you'll like, who know how to reef a sail and steer a course and lay aboard a fat prize with cutlass and pistol."

Terrell finished his eggs and bacon. "Now for those guns," he said, wiping his mouth. "We left three extra six-pounders with you. Where are they?"

"Where but in my magazine behind here?" Colton grinned. "Have all of ye had your fill? Then come along."

He led them through the kitchen, out-of-doors and toward a cluster of sheds beyond. One of these, built of stout old timbers, had a nail-studded door fastened with a gigantic padlock. Colton unfastened this with a brass key and pushed the door inward for them.

The only light came through that door and from a single small window, high up and fitted with a barred grating. The place was full of arms and ammunition. Muskets stood in notched racks, roundshot were set in close order on shelves or stacked in pyramids, powder kegs of all sizes stood one upon the other, all the way to the rafters. And the main floor was occupied by a rank of more than a dozen cannon, each swathed in tarred canvas upon its sturdy carriage.

"I want a lantern to look at these," pronounced Terrell.

"If ye say so, though a spark would blow us all to Cuba," said Colton.

He took a lantern from a peg, stepped outside to light it, and carefully lowered the glass chimney to confine the flame. Back he came with it and held it up as Terrell unlashed the jacket of the nearest gun.

"Here's one of our six-pounders," said Terrell, his gnarled hand stroking the softly shining brass. "Hold that lantern to the muzzle." He peered into the gun. "She's in proper order."

"Aye, for I've taken good care of that gun, and the next two that are also yours," said Colton beside him. "Now, you'll want five more. Look at this beauty."

He handed the lantern to Ranald and pulled the jacket from another gun. The lines of Terrell's face clamped in furious disdain.

"May I eat dirt if that's not the grandfather of all ill weaponry!" he growled. "Poorly cast, poorly bored, and honeycombed with cracks and pits. A single firing would burst it like an egg. I'd not have it for a gift. Ye'd do well to have it forged into saucepans."

Colton cleared other guns of their jackets. Terrell expressed more scorn of several, but finally chose three six-pounders besides those already the property of Haws' party. Then he dipped into a keg of powder, spoke scornfully of its quality and demanded a better article. Orlop Colton was genial, but hard to bargain with. At last Terrell tramped away to arrange the shipping of the guns and ammunition he had approved. Shoup began to ask about recruits for the pirate crew aboard the *Tuscarora*. Ranald strolled out after Terrell.

He gazed to landward, and saw fields for growing of vegetables and Indian corn. Here and there stood trees with trunks and branches that glowed like hot copper. Dark-skinned men in coarse shirts and breeches and straw hats plied hoes among the rows of green growing things. Ranald walked along the row of houses. People stared at him curiously. He saw a ragged little boy, belted with a knife almost as big as himself. Behind the breastwork with its row of cannon lounged its careless guard detail.

He saw Terrell at the end of the dock, waving a red cloth. The *Tuscarora* moved slowly in at the signal, came close to the dock and closer, all its canvas furled except for a jib at the bowsprit. Ranald watched her creep to where she could tie up, and saw a broad gangplank run out. Several of the crew trotted ashore, and followed Terrell back toward Orlop Colton's store.

They returned, trundling one of the six-pounders. The plank creaked as they took it aboard. They went again for the other cannon, one by one. Another party, under direction of Scratch Walker, consulted with Colton, then began to drag stout planks and timbers to the dock.

Examining these, Ranald judged they had been salvaged from wrecks. They were scuffed and beaten, but massive and well-seasoned.

"What do you with these?" inquired Ranald of Walker.

"We'll make this sleek merchantman into a fighting ship," replied Walker. "I'm carpenter of this crew, and we'll have stout bulwarks and gunports ere many hours."

Swiftly the detail worked, with saws, hammers and spikes. The gunwales were built up massively, to the height of a man, except for a single broad opening, like a gateway, to either side. For these gaps, Walker himself sawed planks and nailed them into two doors to hang on hinges. Other men cut the gunports and made hatches to fit them.

They stoutly decked the bow, at the level of the old railing, and there they refitted the bow swivel so as to command the seas, forward and to each side, above the raised defenses. Just aft of this raised gun position they sawed a hatchway in the deck. In the hold beneath they made a powder room, with double-thick walls, and a ladder mounting from its door to the main deck. Into this they moved the powder and small arms and most of the shot. Shotracks at the various gun positions held other shot in readiness.

As the guns were set at their ports and lashed in place, Terrell saw that the touch holes were snugly covered with rounded breech aprons of sheet lead, and tampions fitted into the muzzles like corks into bottles.

Dr. Pilbeam and Cato carefully hoisted the wounded Haws up from the cabin. He half sat, half lay, in a canvas chair, his splinted leg resting on a stool. He looked weak,

but not so pale. And when Ranald approached, he smiled
a greeting.

"The air tastes good, Master Blaikie," he said. "But
you're not out of your duty yet. The doctor says 'twill be
weeks ere I can captain us. How like you Grand Cayman?"

"Not vastly well, sir," admitted Ranald. "They're a
lazy, shiftless population, and keep slovenly guard."

"So I've thought ere this," said Haws. "But yonder
comes Quartermaster Shoup, and with him some new
comrades. Bid him fetch them to me."

Ranald beckoned, and Shoup led a dozen men to stand
respectfully before the captain's chair. Haws questioned
one after another. They looked like rascals, but spoke like
seamen. The most remarkable specimen among them was
the last to be questioned.

He was of little more than medium height, but his
great muscles burst from his ragged shirt sleeves and the
legs of his breeches. His shoulders jutted like cliffs, his
chest was as thick as a waterbutt. His brown face was set
with a hooked nose and deep-set, slanting eyes, his lips
were thin and wide, and his chin looked as hard as an
anvil. He wore his coarse black hair swept back but not
pigtailed, and his brows were bound with a length of
twisted rawhide.

"Zounds, friend, you are thewed like a bull," remarked
Haws. "What's your name?"

"Metoquah," was the deep reply.

"It sounds Indian. Are you a Carib?"

"No." And the great, dark head shook. "Cherokee."

Haws stroked his cheek, where a wound was newly healed. "How did a Cherokee happen to come to Grand Cayman?"

"I swam," said Metoquah. "Jumped from a ship and swam ashore."

"Colton tells me he can serve and aim and fire a cannon," volunteered Shoup.

"And we need gunners," nodded Haws. "Metoquah, count yourself our shipmate. Where's Terrell? Read these men the articles, Terrell, and let them sign."

Watching, Ranald saw that all set a cross to the articles except Metoquah, who was able to sign his name.

The new men were put to work at once. Most of them helped with the carpentry. Two were sailmakers and set to sewing canvas into broad, square topsails to augment the *Tuscarora's* schooner rig. Metoquah, among the carpenters, drew admiring stares as he worked, for his strength was tremendous. He handled great timbers like laths, and drove big spikes with single smashing blows of a hammer. He spoke very little, even when questioned. Only with Cato did he seem to relax and converse.

As for Cato, he had assumed full responsibility as steward of the company. While the carpentry went on for two more days, Cato went ashore to bargain for fresh vegetables. He paid particular attention to big supplies of white potatoes and onions, both of which were grown in gardens inland.

Dr. Pilbeam applauded this. "With fresh food of this sort, we need not expect scurvy among us," he said. "The medical faculty is coming to recognize that."

Shoup found more recruits, too. The ship's company
was increased to forty-four, more than twice the number
that had sailed from Carolina. Some of the newcomers
were evil-looking enough, but all seemed to be fine sailor-
men.

At noon of the third day, Shoup and Harrowby and
Terrell inspected the refitting work aboard and pronounced it adequate. The heightened bulwarks were like
a stout wooden fort, pierced with four gunports to starboard and four more to larboard. Each had a snug hatch-
like covering, and all but two were commanded by six-
pounders. The stout gun carriages, each running upon
four small, broad-tired iron wheels, were lashed with
strong cordage to cleats upon the deck. All pieces were
loaded with powder and shot, and tampions and breech
aprons replaced. Terrell also ordered iron housings on the
bulwarks fore and aft, to either side of the swivels. To
these could be fixed lighter guns, like great bell-mouthed
blunderbusses, for close work with big handfuls of shot.

The whole refashioned hull was painted black, by men
sitting in rope slings, and black paint was put upon the
masts and spars as well. As the finishing touches were
applied, word came up from the cabin where Haws still
spent most of his time.

It was an order for Ranald. The *Tuscarora,* armed and
manned for freebooting adventure, would sail with the
mid-afternoon tide. Ranald was directed to lay a course
south and after a while southeast, for the waters off Cen-
tral America. And lookout was to be kept for Spanish
ships, sailing with rich cargoes for their home country.

# *prize-taking* ⚓6⚓

Away they sailed, all evening and all night and until noon of the next day. Again they had bright weather and a breeze from the west, and the new square-cut topsails were set to profit by it.

Ranald watched the men as they worked on deck and aloft. There was no stern discipline, indeed officers and seamen were on easy, familiar terms. But the recruits were brisk and able, as seemed to be the way with pirates. Best of them all was the sturdy Metoquah. For all his bulk, and Ranald guessed that he must weigh more than two hundred pounds, he climbed the rigging like a squirrel, slid nimbly out on crosstree or gaff to set or trim sails. Though he sprang nimbly to Harrowby's orders, he spoke hardly at all to his superiors or his mates.

"Yonder's a sullen redskin dog," commented Shoup as he steered, with Ranald and Harrowby on the quarterdeck beside the tiller. "He won't even give you an 'aye, aye' when you command him. I wonder if we did well to join him to our fellowship?"

"If you call him a dog, he's a proper mastiff," said Harrowby. "They say he's a good gunner, and a proper salty sailor. I wonder where he learnt seamanship."

"Nay, he'll never tell you that, or aught else of himself," put in Ranald. "Like a clock, he speaks but a word an hour."

"Say rather a sand-glass," Harrowby suggested. "He speaks not at all, only carries out his duty."

They spied no ships at close hand for more than a hundred and fifty miles, only now and then a far glimpse of a sail on the horizon to westward. Such craft must be Spanish, Harrowby and Terrell judged, plying from the region of Honduras toward the western end of Cuba. Ranald heard talk of seeking close quarters with these vessels, but decision was made against it.

"Were Cap'n Haws but hale and on deck, we might seek them out and board them," said Terrell.

"Because he's helpless, must we bide helpless, too?" protested Shoup. "Surely we can sail and fight without him."

"Speak for yourself, Tucker," said Harrowby. "He ordered us to seek rich, easy prey as it comes up from the ports around the Gulf of Darien, and his word is my law, be he on his feet or off them."

By noon of their second day out from Grand Cayman, Ranald set them on a new course, south by southeast. This brought them between the treacherous shoals of

Half Moon Reef and Quita Sueno Bank, near small islands named Providencia and San Andres. There, at Haws' direction, they cruised here and there, quietly and unhurriedly, some two hundred miles or more above the rich Spanish port of Cartagena on the South American mainland.

Cartagena seemed a name of golden glory to the pirates. The oldest of the recruits told Ranald about Cartagena, while his gray beard bristled hungrily.

"Aye, Cartagena was bursting with gold fifty years back," the old fellow remembered. "I was but a boy then, aboard my first ship. But I heard men tell of sailing with Morgan to capture the ships laden with golden plate, enough wealth to ransom King George hisself. And there's still rich spoil to be taken from there, if so be we could fight our way to it."

It was mid-May now, and more than three weeks since Ranald had signed his name to the articles of piracy. Captain Haws had recovered somewhat from his wounds, enough to hobble up on deck with a cane to take weight off his injured leg. Ranald was free, more or less, of his responsibility as Sailing Master, but he was treated as a valued member of the company.

"Sir," he ventured to address Haws one hot morning on the quarterdeck, "I would ask you frankly, what is to be my future? Will you never set me free ashore?"

"I might, were there a shore to which we could come safely and land you with safety to yourself," replied Haws. "Since it's a time of war, we'd do you no kindness landing you just anywhere."

"Suppose you put into a harbor of one of the French islands," Ranald suggested. "I could get a ship there for
Carolina."

"We might do that," Haws agreed. "But aboard a ship
for Carolina, what if you came across Spaniards? They'd
sink your ship, and you, too. Bide with us a space, Master
Blaikie, and you may find it a pleasant life yet."

Just then a cry came from a lookout aloft that a sail
was in sight, and Haws peered toward the far horizon to
northeastward. A square-rigged vessel was there.

"Bring her about, and head for that ship!" Haws commanded the steersman. "Harrowby, Terrell, get the men
to their stations!"

Harrowby blew shrill blasts on his pipe, and there was
swift scurrying. Terrell plunged below decks to the magazine and then scrambled up again, with an armload of
pistols and a sheaf of cutlasses. These he dealt out to the
men, and called for a blanket to be dipped overside for
hanging in the door of the powder room. Then he went
below for more weapons.

Shoup took the tiller and brought the *Tuscarora's* nose
around, to head for the other ship. At Harrowby's orders,
Metoquah and another sailor climbed aloft to put on
every stitch of sail. The *Tuscarora* ran handsomely. She
made considerably more speed than the other vessel,
which became a larger and clearer sight as they approached.

"She's Spanish, true enough, by her lines and rigging,"
said Haws, a glass to his eye. "There's her flag to tell her

nation, too. We'll lay aboard her before another hour is past."

"By your leave, Captain, I'll go below to my cabin," said Ranald. "My duties don't include prize-taking."

"I give no such leave, Master Blaikie," Haws replied shortly. "You'll stay on deck with the rest of us, and see how things are done. As to prize-taking, 'tis a Spaniard we have yonder. Spain is your enemy and mine. We're no worse than any appointed privateer, with letters of marque to plague enemy shipping."

"Aye, but that's war, not cruel crime," Ranald said flatly.

"See how things are done," Haws told him again.

The men were priming the touch holes of the guns with fine powder. The gunners stood, each holding a linstock with match ready lighted and glowing. Nearer they came to the Spanish ship. Ranald, looking beyond the *Tuscarora*'s masts and sails, saw a bustle of men aboard the Spaniard, who seemed to be making excited preparations.

Hawks raked the horizons with his glass. "No companions to her," he said. "She must be a ship inbound from Spain. Harrowby, run up the Jolly Roger."

"Aye, aye, sir!"

Harrowby shook out a great black banner, splotched with white. He hooked it to a dangling halyard and hauled to raise it to the peak of the mainsail gaff. A puff of wind spread out the fabric, and every pirate cheered. The white upon the black showed as the silhouette of a great grinning skull, set above two crossed bones.

Terrell ran along the deck, shouting orders of his own. The gun ports were dragged open and the guns rolled forward to protrude forbiddingly.

Haws put a speaking trumpet to his lips. "To the bow swivel, Gunner Terrell!" he shouted. "Fire a shot across her bows!"

They had approached to within a cable's length of the other ship, which was trying to flee. Terrell scrambled to the raised platform where the bow swivel stood ready. He took a linstock from one of the crew and half-crouched to sight. A motion of his hand, and the swivel was turned a trifle. Leaning as if to sight along the length of the piece, Terrell nodded, moved to stand beside the breech, and put the match to the touch hole.

A bellowed explosion, a great leaping burst of sooty smoke, and the shot went skipping across the waves. It danced ahead of the Spanish ship, a peremptory command to lay to and await the will of the pursuer.

The Spaniard had guns, too, fore and aft, and men stood by them. But nobody trained these pieces toward the *Tuscarora*. After a moment, the sails of the Spaniard slackened as she came about into the wind. Down slid her flag from its masthead. Another cheer from the pirates. The *Tuscarora* sped close to the prey.

They came to close quarters, the bow of one ship opposite the stern of the other. As the *Tuscarora* laid to, the pirate gunners caught up grappling irons fastened to long lean chains, to throw aboard the Spaniard and snatch her close; but before this could happen, while the two hulls were yet a dozen feet apart, Metoquah suddenly sprang to the top of the gunwale, a pistol in his right hand and a cutlass clamped crosswise in his strong teeth. He gave a great flying leap, gained the gunwale of the other ship, and caught the shrouds to swing himself to her deck.

They heard him whoop fiercely. Then the grappling irons were flung, striking their sharp prongs into the timbers of the Spanish ship. The pirates swarmed after Metoquah, cutlasses and pistols in their hands.

Still on the quarterdeck with Haws, Ranald stared intently. The sailors aboard the Spanish vessel seemed to cower, as though already doomed. Surely their blood would flow in a moment. But it was not like that at all.

Harrowby, at the head of the boarding party, spoke in Spanish to the captured men, who moved back to let a richly dressed figure come to the ship's side. At Harrowby's word, this man swung across to the *Tuscarora,* and Haws limped down the steps to the main deck.

"*Buenos dias, Senor Capitan,*" said Haws, as cordially as though they had met at a pleasant social gathering.

"I speak English," replied the other coldly, with a heavy accent.

He was of middle age, elegantly slim, with a sharp, smooth-shaven face and carefully dressed gray hair. His wine-colored coat was heavily laced with gold, and decorated at the collar with pearls. At his belt hung a sword with a jewelled hilt.

"My name is Don Polycarpo Lopez," he said, "and I need not be told yours. You are that bloody pirate Reuben Haws, reported sunk and done for by Don Carlos Montero's frigate *Compeador*. Alas, that it was not true."

"Nay, my life sticks too close for your friends to husk it from me," said Haws, his good humor unabated. "I commend you on your wisdom, Captain, in that you did not try to fight us."

"How fight you?" said Lopez bitterly, and his eyes were like embers burnt deep into his sockets. "My ship *Golondrina* has but two guns, and they were nothing against yours. Now, do promptly what you will do, and no mocking of us. Must we hang or walk the plank?"

"Nay," smiled Haws, "you have submitted, and I'll hurt no man of yours. All we want is what you have of worth aboard you. To begin with, I bespeak that fine coat you wear. It must be the richest garment your *Golondrina* has aboard, and as such belongs to our lookout who sighted you." He turned to where Metoquah stood among the listening pirates. "And you, for being first to set foot on the prize's deck, do you claim his gem-crusted sword?"

Metoquah took a stride forward, drew the blade from its sheath and examined it. Then he shook his head.

"It is small and thin," he said. "Give it to someone else. I'll pick a better weapon."

Meanwhile, Harrowby and Shoup were exploring the captured vessel. It was cargoed with Spanish cloth and canary wine for the colonies. In Captain Montero's cabin was a strongbox full of gold coins and silver pieces of eight. A rich passenger had a leather pouch with another large sum, and here and there jewelled rings and chains and other valuables were also gathered.

Terrell ordered the Spanish seamen to bring the *Golondrina's* cannon aboard. They were fine six-pounders, and would furnish the two empty positions left in the *Tuscarora's* broadsides. Powder and shot, a rack of musket and a number of good Spanish swords were also appropriated. Cato surveyed the provisions and helped himself liberally to them. And Dr. Pilbeam examined a stock of medicines.

"Not as good as English drugs, but better than none," he said, and ordered them taken to his quarters.

The casks of wine were shifted to the *Tuscarora's* hold, along with many bolts of fine silks, brocades and other expensive cloths. This done, Harrowby ordered half a dozen pirates to climb the masts of the *Golondrina*. With their cutlasses they severed the main lines that controlled the sails. When they were done, Haws bowed sweepingly to Lopez.

" 'Twill take you some hours to mend your rigging and get under way again," Haws said. "By then we'll be beyond any pursuit you may bring after us. *Adios,* and come again with more good things for us."

"I tell you to your face, you're a heartless, gallows-cheating monster," Lopez replied fiercely, but Haws only laughed aloud.

"If that were truth, you'd never dare to say it to me," he reminded, "for you'd fear such harsh words would be your last. Come, if you have no better courtesy for us, we'd best part ways."

The ships drew apart again. Ranald heard Metoquah claiming, as his right as first boarder, the best weapon from the prize. He pointed to a heavy boarding axe with an edge whetted to a razor sharpness.

"Nay, wouldn't you rather pick a fine pistol or a bright sword?" asked Terrell.

"The axe is for Indians," insisted Metoquah, and took it up in his huge, dark hand.

The *Tuscarora* made way to northeast. Haws and his subordinates made a study of the plundered valuables, and set aside a certain sum as a company treasury, for expenses of the ship and other matters. What was left came to more than six thousand pieces of eight in value. They counted it out into piles of bright yellow and white metal on the deck. Each pile represented some hundred and twenty pieces of eight.

"To Captain Haws, two shares," pronounced Harrowby, scooping two piles into a canvas bag. "For me as Boatswain, Tucker Shoup as Quartermaster, Terrell as Gunner, Sailing Master Blaikie, and Dr. Pilbeam, a share and a half each. Take them, mates. The other shares go to our company, one to each man."

The pirates lined up happily to receive their money. Harrowby gathered his coins into a big kerchief, Walker filled a gourd bowl with his, Pilbeam used a hat, Shoup a stocking. But Ranald stood motionless and only looked at the heap allotted to him.

" 'Tis fairly yours, youngster," said Haws, leaning on his cane. "Spoil from the enemy, according to our articles. Or do you still turn away, as from blood money?"

"Nay, no drop was shed aboard that Spanish ship," said Ranald. "That's what I think on."

"Why kill helpless men?" asked Haws. "They did not resist, so we took what we wanted and let them go. They will spread the word that we do no foul deeds when there's no use of them."

"I remember when you and your men came aboard the *Tuscarora*," said Ranald. "I bargained with you then. I promised to serve you as Sailing Master, if you would spare my companions."

"And you kept your promise, and signed articles with us," nodded Haws.

"Now I wonder, what if I'd refused to join you?" Ranald demanded. "If I'd defied you to do your worst to me, what would your worst have been?"

Haws laughed aloud. "We'd have just put you in the boat with those others—aye, even the pretty lass, though Scratch Walker wanted to hold her for ransom—and let you row away."

Ranald clenched his fists, but Haws put a hand on his shoulder.

"You acted the brave part that day, not knowing our forbearance," he said. "And we're glad you're one of us, however it came about. Now, take up your prize money."

Cato helped Ranald gather their gold and silver coins and carry them off to their quarters.

# *the promise of freedom* ⚓ **7** ⚓

For days the *Tuscarora* prowled above the Gulf of Darien and the coast of South America, looking for other prey. The great fleets of Spanish ships, cargoed with produce and gold and jewels, had departed for home ports earlier in the spring. In any case, they would have been too much for the *Tuscarora* to attack, for they stayed in close groups and were heavily armed. The pirates hoped for a lone ship, with riches aboard.

In two weeks they spied no other sails except huge ones that indicated tall, dangerous vessels. Haws was almost entirely recovered by now. He directed the course of the *Tuscarora* in person, and Ranald was idle. He began to find pleasure in talking to his shipmates.

Dr. Pilbeam was the most educated man aboard. He lent Ranald books, among them an old favorite, *Robinson Crusoe,* and a volume of Dryden's poems. Harrowby and

Terrell liked to talk with Ranald. Shoup, the Quartermaster, had a fund of exciting stories, both his own adventures and tales about other pirates. Almost the only member of the company who remained aloof was Metoquah. He exchanged few words with anyone except Cato.

"Sooth, Cato, you're remarkable in that you can draw that big Indian into discourse," remarked Ranald one day.

"He speaks to the point when he will," said Cato. "Maybe he seeks me out because once he was a slave like me." Cato reconsidered this. "No, not like me, he was whipped and starved. He says some white men captured him in his own country, the mountains. They sold him to the owner of a ship, who worked him hard and treated him badly. So he jumped off that ship, and swam miles, to Grand Cayman."

"Then he came aboard the *Tuscarora* to be free," Ranald suggested.

"No, Metoquah says no man is free. He says that Captain Haws is bound by the wounds he took. You are bound by your promise to help sail the pirates where they want to go. And the pirates are bound by their thirst for blood and gold."

"Metoquah said that?" asked Ranald, interested. "Then he's a philosopher. He's educated beyond most of these fellows, too—few of them can write their names, and he can. I wonder who taught him to read and write."

"He says he taught himself. He reads whatever he can find to read."

"Then let him have this." Ranald handed Cato the *Robinson Crusoe*. "I know Dr. Pilbeam won't mind. Maybe it will give Metoquah pleasure."

And so, while others of the crew spent their leisure time in lounging, tale-telling, and sometimes playing with dice or cards for the money taken from the *Golondrina*, Metoquah would sit with his broad back against a mast or bulwark or gun carriage, the open book in his hand. His wide, hard lips moved as he spelled out the words of the great castaway adventure.

At the dawn of a day in early June, they found themselves a mile or so from a green-hulled barkentine, with square sails on its foremast and fore-and-aft rig on its mainmast. It flew Spanish colors, and tried to pull away as the *Tuscarora* made for close quarters.

Harrowby piped the men to battle stations. At Haws' word, the black flag was run up. As the *Tuscarora* narrowed the distance, the Spaniard opened fire with her stern gun. The shot went wide, but Haws fairly snarled in fury.

"Musketeers to the crosstrees!" Haws roared through his trumpet. "Trim sails, Harrowby, get to windward of her! Stand by, Terrell, to hull her with a broadside!"

Two parties of men scrambled up the shrouds, with muskets, powder horns and bullet pouches slung to their shoulders. The gun crews mustered at their stations, clearing the breech aprons away and priming the touch holes. Terrell set a string of men to handing up powder bags from below, and went from gun to gun, giving orders.

They were following the Spaniard within a hundred yards by now. Another shot tore through the *Tuscarora's* foresail, but did no other harm. Shoup steered them closely in, to windward of the quarry. Close they drove, and as they approached from larboard, broadside on, Terrell howled the order to fire.

One after another, the starboard guns boomed. Ranald, from the quarterdeck, stared amazed; for so well did the gunners aim that every shot took effect. The cannonballs slammed into the side of the ship opposite, splintering it along the waterline. One ball broke the Spaniard's mainmast. It went overboard with a great splash.

"In! In!" Haws shouted through his trumpet. He hurried down from the quarterdeck. Two pistols dangled from the ends of a sash slung around his neck, and in his right fist he lifted his drawn sword.

But the Spaniard was in poor case to run or fight. Already she heeled over, water pouring through the great holes shot into her side. The dragging mast made it almost impossible for her to steer. As the gun crews loaded again, the musketeers in the crosstrees sent a volley of lead down among the men on the deck opposite.

Then the ships grated together, and the grapnels were flung. The pirate boarders flung themselves from rail to rail. But the Spanish sailors were holding up their hands and howling for quarter. There would be no fighting hand to hand.

Haws sprang aboard the captured vessel. Ranald, close at the rail, heard him speak to the gold-laced Spanish captain who stood before him in terror.

"You were a fool to shoot at us, and I hope you'll profit by your own folly," said Haws. "I've scarce time to tell you more than that. Fetch out your strongbox, and show my Gunner where to find your arms and powder. What's your cargo?"

The ship was laden with tropical woods and tanned ox-hides for shipment to Spain. These bulky things could hardly be taken aboard the *Tuscarora* with any ease and speed. Haws told the Spaniards to launch their boats and get away before the ship sank under their feet. The pirates helped them put water kegs and biscuit bags into the boats, then loosed the grappling irons and returned to the *Tuscarora* with what booty they had been able to find. As the *Tuscarora* sailed away, Ranald watched the laden boats pull clear of the foundering green hull.

"Well, Master Blaikie, that time you saw some shooting," said Haws to him. "Do you feel we acted heartlessly?"

"It strikes me you acted as a privateer might act, and no more," Ranald had to say.

"Aye. The sinking ship yonder is Spanish, your enemy and mine. We've just put a dent in the power of Spain, as though we were any British ship of war."

Ranald watched the sinking wreck. "What if she'd been British, yonder merchantman? Would you have boarded and robbed her?"

"Being pirates, we might have, though not so zestfully as we did."

"Captain Haws," said Ranald, "I'll have no part in action against British vessels."

Haws nodded, almost as though in agreement. "These are war times, and I doubt if you'll find the necessity," he said. "In Spanish waters, we're not apt to find any British save armed, fighting ships. But Harrowby and Shoup count out the money we took. Come along and have your share."

The *Tuscarora* cruised here and there, toward the Bay of Honduras and back off the coast of South America, but found no more victims. Ships went in fleets, too strong to be attacked. At the end of July, Haws set a course northward toward the Windward Passage again, to round the western capes of Haiti and seek a friendly landfall on French Tortuga.

One afternoon in early August, as they passed some seven miles east of a little palm-tufted isle, a great ship cleared that bit of land from behind. She bore huge square sails on three tall masts, and her hull was brilliant red in color. She shifted course and sailed toward them. At once Haws ordered them to put about for the east and run at top speed for Haiti.

"I know that cursed ship, mates," said Terrell, a glass to his eye. "She's the same blood-dyed Spanish frigate that shot us to pieces up yonder on the North Carolina coast. She's the *Compeador*, and the least of her forty-odd guns shoots farther than our best. Would I could drop a red-hot shot into her powder magazine and blow her to every wind that sweeps the sea!"

He handed his glass to Ranald, who looked at the pursuing *Compeador*. Even so far away, she seemed gigantic. Ranald saw that she was built high, both fore and aft,

and that she was running swiftly in a plain effort to over-
take them.

"Up with the French colors!" called out Haws. "And
every rag of canvas we have, crowd it on!"

Metoquah was swift to jump to that order. Shoup, at
the tiller, set them due east, and the sails were set to
catch every possible advantage of the wind. Terrell
sprang to another order from Haws, clearing the stern
gun for action. Harrowby came to join Haws and Ranald
on the quarterdeck.

"Forty miles to the Haitian coast, Captain," he reported, "and we're making good speed of it, ten miles an
hour as I judge."

"How far behind us is that Spanish frigate, think you?"
Haws asked him. "I would say five miles."

Harrowby peered at the distant pursuer, first under his
shading palm, then through a glass. "Five miles, or
nearly," he agreed. "And see to her, she too is rigged out
with every sail in her locker. She's gaining on us, a
little."

For some time they fled, studying the Spaniard. Haws
and Harrowby and Shoup reckoned that the enemy was
making eleven yards to the *Tuscarora's* ten, closing the
gap gradually but inexorably.

"Then from here to Haiti 'twill be nip and tuck," announced Haws.

"Pray heaven it won't be tuck instead of nip," mumbled
Shoup.

Four months at sea had fouled the hull of the *Tuscarora* somewhat, and some of the pirates moaned aloud,

wishing they had careened and scraped away the weeds.

On into the afternoon the race continued. As the Spaniard came closer, signals were flown to tell the *Tuscarora* to wait and exchange messages, but these were ignored. It was nearly four o'clock when the forward lookout cried out that land showed on the horizon.

"Haiti is yonder," said Haws.

"And dangerous shoal waters," added Harrowby.

"No more danger than that Spanish frigate," said Haws. "Shoup, you know these coasts. Put us in where that red devil dare not follow."

As Shoup obeyed, skilfully steering them among rocks and bars, the Spaniard was close enough to try shots from three bow guns, but these went harmlessly wide. Leadsmen at the bow of the *Tuscarora* kept sounding for bottom and crying out that it was no more than a fathom and a half. Once or twice the keel seemed to scrape slightly.

"They wanted to sink us, and that most earnestly," commented Haws, gazing out to sea where the *Compeador* was forced to stay in deep water. "Yet we have French colors up, and should be safe."

"They know who we are," said Shoup darkly, as he steered. "That fellow Lopez, whom we spared and let sail away, must have borne word of us. Now that word hath come back to Cuba. They know our description, from waterline to masthead."

"We escaped, however," reminded Haws.

"Had we sunk those ships we took, with all aboard, no warning of us would have been carried," Shoup said.

"Dead men tell no tales, Blackbeard was wont to say."

"But Blackbeard was taken and slain at last, and his head cut off for a show," put in Terrell. "We're in a chancey trade, mates, however we treat captives. Where away now, Cap'n?"

Haws kept them close to the shore of Haiti, and they did not slide out of shallow water until sundown. They kept to westward of the island of La Gonave, and by morning rounded a cape, to come in the afternoon of the following day to Tortuga.

There they anchored in a pleasant bay among French ships, and were welcomed ashore in the town among the palms. Haws was greeted by a government officer, who spoke in a swift rattle of French. Others of the pirate crew hurried into seaside taverns where they, too, seemed to meet friends.

"Tortuga was ever a kindly haven for our sort," Harrowby told Ranald. "Many here are children of the stout old Brethren of the Coast—the buccaneers who first hunted wild cattle on Haiti and sold the hides and flesh, then hunted the ships that hunted them. That officer who speaks to our Captain would never do us ill, except perhaps in a trade."

But no trading was done. The French storekeepers quoted low prices for the casks of wine, saying that they were well supplied. Nor did they make what Haws considered a reasonable offer for the bolts of fine cloth. Haws called his company back on board after two days in port.

"Weigh anchor at dawn," he said. "We'll sail east of the

Bahamas and so up to Topsail Inlet. There we'll get better prices than here on Tortuga."

Ranald pricked up his ears at the name of Topsail Inlet. It was at the southern end of the North Carolina coast, not unthinkably far from his home.

Away they sailed, northward with a brisk wind astern. Now they flew British colors, and passed islands and vessels unchallenged. An eight days' voyage presented neither dangers nor great labors. At last they approached the mainland, and Shoup steered them through an inlet between sandy outer banks to the shore beyond.

They anchored in the morning, off a beach of sandy dunes, with thickets of tall, dark pines farther inland. A great house stood there, with a low-eaved roof of planks and two big stone chimneys. Around it were grouped smaller sheds and cabins, and people came from them, as at Grand Cayman, to see boats put off from the *Tuscarora*.

Ranald was in the same boat with Haws. As it beached, a plump, grizzled man in loose shirt and breeches, with iron-buckled shoes, came forward. He held a straw hat in one hand and offered the other to Haws in welcome.

"Master Blaikie, this is our friend, Jacob Tomlinson," said Haws. "Are you still in the free trade, Jacob? We have wine and silks and satins aboard, at reasonable prices. And we'd like to careen and refit."

"Do so, Captain Haws," said Jacob Tomlinson. "Will you come indoors to talk business? The tide's on its way in, and your ship can beach handily."

Dr. Pilbeam went with Haws and Tomlinson into the big house. Ranald and others of the boat's party watched as the tide fetched the *Tuscarora* in. Then the tide began to recede, leaving the *Tuscarora* ashore. From the big house came two men in shabby sea clothes, bearing bundles of what looked like stores for a voyage. They launched what looked like an old longboat, decked fore and aft, with a mast and a big triangular mainsail and a jib. Within minutes they went sailing away toward the inlet.

As the *Tuscarora* began to settle, Harrowby and others carefully put stakes so that she would not lie wholly upon her side. Ropes from her masts and rails on the opposite side were made fast to trees. Then the pirates gathered, with scrapers set on long handles, to assault the great beardlike tufts of weed and barnacles that clung to the planks below the water line.

When one whole side of the ship was cleared and rubbed smooth with great flat chunks of sandstone, Harrowby and Shoup and Walker sought for traces of worm-tunnelling and other weakness. Several seams were tightly caulked and painted over. Then the whole side below the water line was plentifully coated with hot tar.

"Better than the wax or tallow they use in the West Indies," Walker said to Ranald.

The tide rose anew and covered this work. That night the pirates mostly lay ashore, in the cabins of friends or in hammocks slung between trees. Dawn came, and another ebb of the tide. The *Tuscarora* was canted and braced in the opposite direction, and her other side industriously scraped, searched and tarred.

Meanwhile, negotiations went on in Jacob Tomlinson's house. Haws emerged to say that he was satisfied with terms for the wine and cloth. Those things were fetched from the *Tuscarora* to Tomlinson's storage rooms, the money paid down for them. The pirate company gathered on an open stretch of sand while the shares were counted out and distributed.

Late that night, the sailboat sent out earlier returned. Its two occupants went for a conference with Haws, Dr. Pilbeam and Tomlinson. Ranald slept in his cabin aboard the refloated *Tuscarora*. In the early morning, Harrowby wakened him to say that Haws desired his presence ashore.

"So, Master Blaikie," the Captain greeted him as he set foot on the beach. "You are so near home here, and yet so far."

"I might have slipped away into the woods had I not passed my word," said Ranald.

"You might have done so, and found yourself hopelessly lost amid swamps and marshes," said Haws. "Now hark you well, you've done useful and honest duty with us. Would you like indeed to go back to your people?"

"More than anything else, sir," said Ranald.

"I thought as much. Did you mark a small boat that went from here, and returned last night?"

"Aye, something of the sort," answered Ranald. "I gave it no great attention."

"That boat carried a message to Edenton," Haws told

him. "You know that our Doctor is in want of good drugs and instruments aboard us. So he sent to Edenton, asking a trusted friend to gather a stock of such things. Back came word that it was being done."

"Aye, Captain, and then?" Ranald prompted.

"Why, Dr. Pilbeam goes today to buy his medicines in Edenton," said Haws. "I believe you said you had friends there. So give us your word once again, not to betray where we are for twenty-four hours after you're left in Edenton. If you swear to that, I'll send you with Pilbeam, to be free forever of us pirates and perhaps to forgive us for holding you so long."

# *a new captivity* | ⚓8⚓

In something like a foggy dream of joy, Ranald thanked Captain Haws, made the requested pledge, and asked if Cato, too, would be allowed to go home.

"Aye, and he is coming now to help you pack what things you can take," said Haws. "You have a bag of silver and gold, from our successes against the Spaniards. Of your clothing choose out the best, for the shallop will not carry any great load. Say farewells now, for Dr. Pilbeam is eager to launch for the journey to Edenton."

Edenton—Ranald could not but think of Enid Mandeville. The pirates gathered on deck for friendly leave-takings. Terrell wrung Ranald's hand and wished him eternal good fortune. Harrowby, in parting, praised Ranald's skill at navigation. Shoup also offered compliments. Meanwhile, Dr. Pilbeam had asked for Metoquah to help on the coastwise journey northward. Metoquah and Cato stocked the little shallop with a breaker of fresh water, some corn bread and slices of cold roast meat. Ranald packed a valise with his most valued personal possessions, and Cato brought their prize money in a canvas bag and a parcel of his own things. The four pushed their craft out to deep water and set brisk sail, amid shouted hopes of good fortune for them.

Ranald was steersman. He piloted them out at Topsail Inlet, then called for a shift of sail to take them away northeastward along the Outer Banks. A wind from the south sped them swiftly and smoothly. The clear sky and the bright waters helped make the sail a pleasant one.

Ranald knew these regions from boyhood voyages along the coast. He kept the shallop within view of the Outer Banks to westward. According to a compass set into the thwart beside him, they travelled in a generally northeasterly direction. Dr. Pilbeam sat forward, gazing across the waves. Cato talked for a while with Metoquah, then moved aft to join Ranald.

"It'll be good to be home," said he. "We've been gone only from April to August, but it seems years."

"Aye," Ranald agreed. He thought again of Edenton, and of Enid Mandeville who lived there.

It was past noon when they approached Cape Lookout. They saw ships and some smaller fishing craft in those waters, but none paid them attention.

"They don't look on us as possibly strange or perilous," remarked Pilbeam. "We're only a cockleshell, too small even to fly a flag. How far have we come on our journey?"

"Some sixty miles," estimated Ranald, moving the tiller to shift course a trifle westward and so round the cape. " 'Tis another sixty, I judge, to Hatteras, and a hundred and twenty more beyond that to Edenton."

"Jacob Tomlinson's cunning sailors must have sailed night and day without stopping to make the trip so fast," Pilbeam said. "But they know the way blindfold. We'll do well to come ashore somewhere at dark, and rest the night, then go on tomorrow."

They cut bread and meat for their noonday meal, and kept on northward during the afternoon. Ranald fetched them through Hatteras Inlet and to the western beach of the long bank by sunset. They dragged the boat well up on shore and made it fast to a scrubby tree. Then they gathered wood for a small fire, and sat around it to eat supper like boys on a holiday.

"Upon my soul, this food is the more savory when I think I'm on the good earth of North Carolina," remarked Pilbeam as he munched. "And you, too, are North Carolinian, Master Blaikie, and so is your man Cato. When it comes to that, I think that so is Metoquah."

"Cherokee," said Metoquah in his deep voice. "My people live far off in the mountains."

"Mayhap you'd like to go looking for them," suggested Pilbeam, but Metoquah shook his great head.

"Gone too long," he said. "Many years."

"None would know you?" Ranald asked.

"Not how I am now," Metoquah replied. "I was stolen when I was young. Made to work for white men— learned to read and write, to sail on deep water, fire big guns. Maybe I forget how to spear fish and hunt deer."

"Then come back with me to our roving comradeship, and welcome," Pilbeam said to him.

The moon came up, less than half full. They wrapped themselves in cloaks to sleep on the sand. At dawn they were up, shoving the boat back into the water and setting sail to make their way on the broad expanse of Pamlico Sound.

Ranald's watch showed him that it was not much past six when they started this stage of the journey. They ate breakfast as they travelled. Shortly after nine o'clock they approached the strait between Roanoke Island and the mainland to the west. Croatan Sound, that strait was called. As Ranald steered them through he remembered the story of the first effort of the British to settle on Roanoke Island, and of how their settlement strangely vanished and was never heard of again.

They came to shore and rested a while at the top of Roanoke Island. Then on into Albemarle Sound they plied their way, slowed up because they must tack against a west wind. As the sun was setting they approached the long row of docks at Edenton.

Ship after ship lay moored there, with others anchored farther out in the sound. Beyond the masts and the piers rose the colonial capital of North Carolina, waterfront stores and taverns and pleasant houses.

Pilbeam posted himself at the bow to guide Ranald's steering.

"Here, in close between these two ships, and we'll tie up," he said at last. "This dock belongs to Matthew Tilford. I know him well, and he expects me at his tavern."

They made fast and mounted to the broad planks above.
The waterfront street showed lamplighted windows. People walked on the brick pavement, but none paid attention as Pilbeam led his party along. At the corner of a
cross street he motioned for a halt, and looked in at the
open door of a tavern.

"Around to the back door, Cato and Metoquah," he
said. "You, Master Blaikie, come in here with me."

They entered a spacious room. Men sat at tables here
and there, eating or drinking or smoking long clay pipes.
Pilbeam and Ranald found a table near the rear wall. A
plump, aproned man approached them.

"Good even to you, Mr. Tilford, and you needn't speak
my name," said Pilbeam quietly. "Your note said you'd
expect me, and that my friend Allenby would meet me
here when I came."

"Aye, he is even now in my kitchen," said the landlord.

"Then I'll go to him there," said Pilbeam, rising.
"There are two men with us, already at your back door.
Will you give them wine? And Master Blaikie will wait
here, and perhaps have some supper."

A waiter came, and Ranald ordered food and drink,
while Pilbeam strolled away and through the kitchen
door.

Alone at the table, Ranald found himself able to enjoy
a good meal. He thought of his prospects with glowing
relish.

He had given his word to keep silence for twenty-four
hours, and perhaps he would be well advised to fetch his
luggage back to this very tavern. He could stay the night,
and the next day, too. By evening of that next day he

would be free of his pledge. He could go and seek out the Mandeville home. Maybe Enid would greet him at the door . . .

As he finished a slice of fruit tart, Dr. Pilbeam returned from the kitchen.

"All is accomplished," he said as he sat down. "Waiter, fetch me something to eat—just what my young friend had will serve."

The waiter departed to fulfill the order. Ranald thought that two men at the table across the room were gazing fixedly at him and Pilbeam. But surely they could not hear anything across the floor.

"My friend Allenby had fetched a fine, well-filled medicine chest, and his price was reasonable," Pilbeam said. "I told Cato and Metoquah to bear it to our boat, and that we'd come later to take out your luggage and bid you farewell."

He poured wine into his glass from the bottle on the table. The waiter came with his supper.

"This will be farewell, I suppose," Pilbeam said. "I, for one, will be sorry to see you no more. I've enjoyed your conversation, and admired your seamanship."

"Let me say honestly that I cannot but wish you well as we part," said Ranald.

"A toast, then, to better times for both."

But as they lifted their glasses to pledge each other, two figures appeared to loom above the table. They were the two men who had stared earlier. Just now they seemed grim and tight-mouthed.

"Upon my soul," said one, "I take this man for Pilbeam,

the renegade and enemy of his own people, who hath cheated the gallows these twenty years."

Ranald felt as though his blood had turned to ice. Dr. Pilbeam only squinted mildly at the two men, above his spectacles.

"You are mistaken, sir," he said mildly. "My name is Harris."

"Nay," said the man who had spoken, and shook his powdered head. He was a tall, middle-aged man in a coat of military cut. "For all the passage of time, I know you, and you know me, too. I am Beckstead, of the militia. I was Ensign when last we were together. I am Captain now."

Ranald started to rise, but the other man whipped out a pocket pistol. "Keep your seat," he warned. "One false move, and 'twill be your last."

The whole roomful of customers was staring. "Why, Captain Beckstead, what's toward?" one asked.

"I have just recognized a scoundrelly outlaw," said Beckstead over his shoulder. "Will one of you go summon the man on watch at the jail, and another carry the news to Magistrate Smithers?"

Two men were up from their chairs and out of the door at once. Beckstead glared again at Pilbeam, then at the wan-faced host, Tilford.

"And so you give entertainment to gallows birds, do you, Mr. Tilford?" he challenged.

Ranald heard Dr. Pilbeam laugh, as though in bitter scorn.

"Egad, I had thought I was in a house where none remembered me," he said, loudly enough for all to hear. "Tilford—is that your name, mine host? I suppose you knew who I was, and betrayed me."

"Nay, sir, you're a stranger to me," spluttered Tilford, masking his gratitude at this trick to exonerate him.

Beckstead's companion still held his pistol ready. "And who are you, you young rascal?" he addressed Ranald.

"Since you're taking us before a Justice, I'll wait and talk to him," said Ranald.

There was a long, tense wait. Then a stout man in a red coat entered, holding a heavy musket at the ready.

"What's the trouble?" he bawled.

"You came promptly, Jailer Spode." Captain Beckstead said to him. "I've asked Mr. Smithers, the Justice, to meet us at our little refuge for transgressors, for here we have notorious ill-doers. Stand up, Pilbeam. You also, whatever your name is. Raise your hands."

Everyone gazed in rapt interest as Pilbeam and Ranald got to their feet. The man named Spode stood with poised musket while Beckstead ran his hands over their bodies and took from Pilbeam a loaded pistol and from Ranald a sheath knife.

"Now, march!" he snapped, like an officer giving commands.

As Spode and Beckstead conducted their prisoners from the tavern, several others made as if to follow, but Beckstead crisply ordered them back. Along the dark street the four walked in silence. They turned at a corner to walk up a rise, and on to where a two-story wooden structure loomed in the night. Ranald recognized it for the courthouse. Spode and Beckstead conducted them around this building to a smaller one behind. Lamplight shone through the open door. When they entered, a grossly fat man in a tight blue coat greeted them.

"What's all this brabble that fetches me from my home, Captain Beckstead?" he asked. "Violence and arrest is all I have heard. Who are these men?"

"One is Rufus Pilbeam, a known rogue, Your Worship," replied Beckstead. "Long hath he been sought by officers of the law, for aiding savage Indians against our colony. At first he denied his name, but then confessed to it. This other was with him in Tilford's tavern when I accused him."

Briefly he related the circumstances. The fat man listened, then gazed at Ranald.

"Well, young sir?" he prompted. "Who are you? I am Justice Smithers, and I command you to speak the truth."

"My name, sir, is Ranald Blaikie, and I am a native of Bath," Ranald said. "I have lately been a captive of pirates, as I can show by certain witnesses—"

"I'll be a witness," put in Dr. Pilbeam. "We took him into our crew in exchange for freeing his sailors."

"Silence," the Justice snapped at Pilbeam. "Say on, Ranald Blaikie, if that is truly your name. If you were an escaped captive, why did you sit at ease with this accused lawbreaker in the tavern?"

"So please Your Worship, I was not yet free from my captivity," Ranald tried to explain. "I was under parole to keep silent for twenty-four hours after being released."

"Meanwhile, it seems that you drank and made merry with a captor, who should rather have been your foe," said the Justice with a scowl. "That's a strange story, I make bold to observe."

"It's a true one," Ranald insisted.

"Hmmm," grunted the Justice. "Who are these pirates you say held you captive, and where may we find and seize them?"

Ranald was silent.

"Speak when you're questioned," commanded Captain Beckstead.

"I am sworn not to speak," said Ranald. "I've given my word to keep silence for twenty-four hours."

"Hmmm," said the Justice again. "This may be a deep matter, one for the attention of Governor Johnston himself. Lock them up, Spode, and we'll have more to say to them at sunrise. Mayhap they'll be readier to inform us by then, if they hope to save their necks."

Spode unlocked a heavy door at the rear. "In with you," he growled, and when Pilbeam and Ranald had entered the dark chamber beyond, he shut the door behind them. They heard the grating of the huge lock as it was fastened.

The cubicle where they stood was small and hot, with only the dimmest wash of moonlight through a barred window at the back. Ranald groped along a wall. It seemed to be made of massive squared timbers, set together with lime plaster as hard as stone. There was no furniture, only a litter of musty straw in one corner.

"How do we get out of this?" he asked Dr. Pilbeam.

"I fear there's only one road," was the doleful reply. "And that will be a short road indeed, with a long rope waiting at its end."

# *rescue* ⚓9⚓

Ranald unbuttoned his coat and loosened his stock. He felt his way to a corner, and stooped to touch the floor with his hand. It was made of massive planks.

"Here," said Dr. Pilbeam, "I've found a pitcher of water. Will you drink?"

"Thank you, Doctor." Ranald took the pitcher and put it to his lips. The water was warm and stale, but it seemed clean. He passed the pitcher back, and moved to the dim oblong of the window.

He strained his eyes and felt with his hands. The window was perhaps two feet high and three wide, and was set with five upright bars, stoutly made of iron. The waning moon showed a grassy yard outside, and dark houses farther away.

"Maybe we can get out here," he said, and Dr. Pilbeam joined him.

A more careful examination showed that the window

was defended with a grid. The stout bars were welded into a rectangular frame of heavy wrought iron. It was tightly fitted in the window hole, fastened there with bolts driven into the timbers of the wall. That stony plaster sealed it massively into place, all the way around. Ranald grasped the bars in his hands and tried to shake them, but they did not even creak.

"They are set as though they grew there," Ranald said.

"Alack, my young friend, I seem to have drawn you with me into destruction," said Pilbeam gloomily. "We're as good as dead, both of us."

"Nay, Doctor, never say that," Ranald tried to rally him. "Pirates win clemency now and then, I have heard say."

"Aye, but it's not as a pirate they hold me," Pilbeam rejoined. "You heard those charges against me—traitor and renegade."

"I'll never believe such things of you."

"Hark you to what happened, and tell me then if there's a chance of survival."

Pilbeam lowered himself to sit in a corner. "Don't sit on the straw, it will be filthy," he cautioned.

Ranald too, sat down, just under the barred window. "I am ready to listen," he said.

"Early in the century there were Indian wars," Pilbeam began. "The Tuscarora tribe—the brave people whose name you gave your ship—fought the settlers to west and north of here, but at last they themselves were beaten and driven."

"I've heard somewhat of that Tuscarora War," remarked Ranald.

"Then more settlers came and made homes along the Roanoke River," Pilbeam continued. "I was young then, and eager to be useful as a man of medicine. I went to that country, I built myself a house, and the others made me welcome." Soft moonlight touched Pilbeam's glasses. "I cured fevers and helped babies into the world. Some Indians still clung to their old home country, and I did what I could for them, too, when they were sick."

"And kindly done, sir," Ranald said.

"Some of the settlers thought otherwise. Well, a score of years back, those Indians tried to fight the white men again. It was no great war, for they were few. They killed several farmers and burned a house or two. The militia mustered to wipe the Indians out."

The Doctor paused, as though remembering. "Then, sir?" Ranald asked after a moment.

"I did not even know of these things at first, for the fighting did not come near me. But one morning, two Indian hunters I knew crept to my door. They had been shot and sorely wounded. I fetched them in, took the bullets from their wounds, and bandaged them. But one was too lame and weak to move, and his friend stayed by him, to take care of him. That same day, a file of men with muskets came. They were commanded by the same man who accused me tonight."

"You mean Captain Beckstead," said Ranald.

"Aye, Beckstead. He was a young Ensign of militia then. He knocked with the butt of his pistol to summon me. His men were chasing Indians, and had seen moccasin tracks on the trail, with blood to make the way clearer. They ordered me to surrender any Indians I might have in my house, to be killed outright."

"And that you could never do," said Ranald.

"No." Pilbeam's voice sounded tired. "I lied to those militia. I said that I was alone in my house. But they pushed their way inside, and dragged out my two patients. They shot them dead in my front yard. Beckstead accused me of treason, of siding with the Indians to massacre my own people."

Ranald shook his head in the dark. "What reply did you make to that, sir?"

"The worst possible reply. I cursed them for murderers and men of blood. Beckstead told me I was under arrest. But when one of the militiamen took hold of me, I knocked him down, ran out and rode away on one of their own horses. They followed, and somehow I lost them in the woods. Then I came my way here to Edenton. 'Twas only a little huddle of houses by the water in those days. I got aboard a trading sloop and sailed down to Charleston ere orders for locking me up followed me. But I heard that I was proscribed as an outlaw, that my life was forfeit if I were captured. I fled again, to Florida and at last to Havana, out of reach of this colony's law."

"And became a pirate," supplied Ranald.

"There was naught else for me. I met Captain Haws, who was there in port to find men for his company. He and I found reasons to like each other, and I became Doctor aboard his ship, and so I have served ever since."

He was silent again, as though his story was finished.

"You say you like Captain Haws," said Ranald. "I can say the same, I think, though I know very little of who and what he may truly be."

"And I know little more than you," said Pilbeam. "Only that he is a bold man of the sea, with gentle manners, and that he is both fair and kind as pirates go. I know that much, and that Haws is not his real name."

"At least Cato and Metoquah escaped," said Ranald, trying to sound cheerful. "They'll sail back to Topsail Inlet and tell what happened. Who knows? Haws may well come here and win us free somehow."

"I don't doubt but that he'll try," agreed Pilbeam, with no hope in his own voice. "Yet by then we'll be sped. They'll hang me out of hand, tomorrow or next day, if I know them at all. And since you were taken with me, they'll hang you on the same gallows."

Ranald thought that what Pilbeam said had the sound of a melancholy truth. He found the pitcher on the floor and drank again, to moisten his dry lips.

They were shut up for the night in this stuffy prison, with massive bars on the window and a heavy lock on the door. Morning would see them before a stern judge, and Pilbeam undoubtedly was right about the small chance for mercy, for even sensible justice, in their trial. After that trial, what? A platform, a rope around the neck?

"Well, then," he said aloud, "if die I must, I'll die as bravely as I can."

Then he started violently, for something clinked on the

bars of the window above his head. Instantly he was on his feet. "What was that?" he demanded.

"Softly, Master Ranald," whispered a voice outside. "This is Cato. Don't speak above a whisper."

Ranald turned and shoved his face close to the bars. He could see the dark silhouette of Cato's head, just beyond.

"Don't be a fool," Ranald said under his breath. "You and Metoquah should be making all speed away, for your very lives."

"No," said Cato. "We're going to get you and Dr. Pilbeam out of this jail."

Pilbeam was also at the window. "How, get us out?" he asked. "Why, 'tis impossible."

"Nothing is impossible," said a new voice from outside, and Ranald's heart leaped.

"Enid Mandeville," he almost moaned in despair. "You should never be here, Enid. You must not involve yourself. Go rather, and say to your father—"

"My father is not in Edenton, Ranald."

Enid had replaced Cato at the window. Ranald saw her dark outline close to him.

"My father is not here," she said again. "When the *Tuscarora* was stolen, your father and he found another ship, and he sailed for England. So there was only I at home when Cato came to tell me that he had heard you were taken. We're here to set you free, Ranald."

She put her hand between the bars to take his. Her grasp was firm and steady.

"Free," said Pilbeam after her. "But how can you hope to set us free?"

"I've brought my horse Capulet. He's stout and willing. Here, Cato, Metoquah—where is that hide rope?"

Stealthy, busy sounds came from outside. Peering in the soft wash of moonlight, Ranald saw the horse, with two forms busy at its flanks. The slim one was Cato, the powerful body was Metoquah.

"They're rigging a harness," whispered Enid. "We'll make it fast to these bars. Then Capulet will drag them out of the window and you can come through."

Metoquah approached. Quickly he lashed the ends of the two ropes to bars, side by side at the center. He tugged powerfully to make the knots snug.

"Now," he grunted.

Enid went to the horse's head. "Come up," she commanded, dragging at the reins.

The horse surged forward. The thick leather ropes drew so taut that they hummed, but the iron grid stayed solidly in its fastenings.

"It's too much even for a horse," said Pilbeam.

"Wait," said Metoquah.

He fetched another end of rope and attached it to a third bar. Then he moved clear of the window and drew the other end of the rope after him. Ranald watched as Metoquah wrapped a turn of the line around his hips and braced his feet.

"Now," he said again.

Enid grasped the horse's bridle and pulled on it. The horse threw his weight into the rough harness, and

Metoquah exerted his great strength. The frame of the grid seemed to creak, but it did not move.

They relaxed their efforts. Metoquah stood easy with the rope still looped around him. Enid came close to the bars.

"Did we loosen it?" she asked.

"I heard the thing stir," Ranald replied, "but it is still strongly in place. Enid, I pray you to go, you and Cato and Metoquah. Leave us. You may be trapped here at any moment."

"I won't go away," she said stubbornly. "Nay, take heart, Ranald. All will be well."

"Please, Enid—"

"You saved me once," she cut him off, "and I will save you. We have only to pull more strongly."

Turning from the window, she spoke to Cato.

"Take Metoquah around the waist and be ready to help," she directed. "Ranald, you and your friend inside must push outward on those bars when I give the word. Push with every ounce of your strength."

"Brave lass," said Pilbeam. "By heaven, young Master Blaikie, she may have the right of it. Take your place at one side, and I'll push at the other."

Ranald seized the bar next to the right side of the window with both his hands. He planted his feet apart and gathered all his sinewy muscles for a supreme effort. At the other side, Dr. Pilbeam stationed himself. Ranald saw Enid coax her horse forward to tighten the harness again. Metoquah faced toward the window, made two turns of his own line around his hips and caught hold with his powerful hands. Cato came up behind Metoquah and twined his arms around Metoquah's body.

"Pull," came Enid's low, emphatic command.

She twitched the bridle. Obediently the horse strove. Metoquah threw himself backward, struggling. Cato dragged on Metoquah. Ranald and Pilbeam shoved desperately on the bars they held.

There was a sullen, grinding noise, all around the outside rim of the grid.

"More! More!" Enid cried out, forgetting the need for silence.

She let go the bridle, came along the flank of the horse and slapped the laboring rump with her hand. With a flutter of skirts she ran to the outer line of the harness, seized it in both her hands and pulled with all her might.

With a rattling crash of drawn bolts, the whole grid started from its bed. Next moment it snatched away from Ranald's fingers. He fell against the sill. Outside he saw the horse, Enid, Metoquah and Cato, almost falling away from their own supreme hauling effort.

"What are you doing in there?" bawled the voice of Jailer Spode from within. The lock rattled as though he was trying to fit the key into it.

Unceremoniously, Ranald caught Pilbeam around the waist, lifted him bodily and thrust him into the gap where the grid had been. The Doctor struggled to get through. Ranald shoved, fairly catapulting him into the open. Again Spode yelled at the inner door. Ranald heard the lock groan as it opened. He dived out headfirst as if it were a pool of water, just as the door opened behind him.

He landed on his hands and knees in the gravel, but he was up and running next instant. Ahead of him hurried the others. The barred grid went bouncing and clanging behind Enid's loping horse. As Ranald sped to catch up, he saw Metoquah stooping in mid-stride, a knife in his hand. Two swift, powerful slashes, and Metoquah cut the grid loose to lie on the ground. They all dashed away into an alley. Behind them the Jailer was yelling stridently for help.

The alley was narrow and silent and shadowed. Cato halted the horse and stroked its neck and head to gentle it. Enid caught Ranald by his elbow.

"Cato says you have a boat down at the docks," she said. "Go along this way to the street beyond, and so down to where you can set out over the waters to safety."

"You were braver than a lioness," Ranald assured her.

"Aye, and wiser than an owl," put in Dr. Pilbeam. "We owe you our lives."

"I owed mine to Ranald," Enid said. "He delivered me out of the hands of bloody pirates last spring. He stayed prisoner among them so that I might go free."

Ranald thought of what Captain Haws had said about that bargain, but said nothing.

"Goodbye, Ranald," Enid said to him. "I will be all right when you go—nobody will suspect me of having a hand in your escape. We'll meet again in a good hour, I know."

"I'll pray for that good hour to come soon," Ranald assured her.

Ranald took both her hands in his, leaned close, and kissed her. Then Enid fairly pushed him away and took the horse's bridle once more. She led the horse swiftly out of the alley.

Ranald and Pilbeam hurried after Metoquah and Cato. The four came into the street and turned in the direction of the waterfront. They moved at a brisk but casual walk, as though they were peaceable townsfolk. Several men passed them, but none challenged.

They came to the docks. The broad planks echoed dully beneath their feet as they walked to where the shallop was moored.

Swiftly they got in, untied the line and shoved out. A bit of wind stirred in the night, and Metoquah set the sail to catch it. Ranald took the tiller and steered them into the open sound under the dim light of that scrap of moon.

# *cato's warning* | ⚓ **10** ⚓

Once out upon the broad waters of Albemarle Sound, Ranald headed them west. He told Cato to light a lantern and hang it at the bow, to make them look like any ordinary night-going fisherman or freighter. He did not set a light by the compass, but reckoned their course by the stars. The light of the moon was enough for him to find a safe way.

By midnight they had turned south, to negotiate the Strait of Croatan past Roanoke Island, and into Pamlico Sound. Ranald had sailed so often there that he could steer almost by instinct. He kept the tiller for hour after hour, though both Cato and Metoquah offered to relieve him. The night flowed past, and the miles. The sun came up and showed them the way through Hatteras Inlet.

Ranald felt dull and shaky from his long stretch of piloting duty. He gave the tiller to Cato and drank from the

water breaker. He ate of the dry corn bread and the cold
meat. Then he almost fell flat in the bottom of the boat
and went instantly to sleep.

He woke at noon, to find that his companions had
rigged a bit of canvas above him, to shelter him from the
bright sun. They were approaching Cape Lookout.

"I'll steer again," said he, and relieved Metoquah at the
tiller. "Now we go southwest, and perhaps we can take
advantage of this wind from eastward. We'll get this boat
back to Topsail Inlet as fast as did those men of Jacob
Tomlinson's, maybe faster."

Pilbeam was rummaging the chest of medical supplies
they had brought from Edenton. "A fine selection, and
I'm glad for it," he reported. " 'Twill help us in our voyages."

"I am glad, too, since I'll be on those voyages hence-
forth," said Ranald.

Pilbeam glanced up above his spectacles. "I give you
the words of that brave girl who drew us out of jail," he
said gently. "Take heart, all will yet be well."

"I try my best, Doctor," Ranald said. "Yet 'tis a sad
thought that I cannot go home again."

"I know. I've thought that very thing these twenty
years. But still I don't despair wholly."

"Then neither shall I despair," Ranald promised both
Dr. Pilbeam and himself.

They entered Topsail Inlet by half-past four.

The *Tuscarora* was afloat again, and anchored offshore.
As the shallop came to the beach, both pirates and the

people of the settlement hurried to greet it. Captain Haws came, his face blank with surprise.

"You came back to us," he hailed Ranald. "Why?"

The story of the Edenton adventure was soon told by Dr. Pilbeam, with high praise for Ranald's behavior and for Enid Mandeville's help. The pirates clustered around to hear.

"Sink me," declared Scratch Walker when Pilbeam had finished the telling. "Sink me without trace, mates, but I feel I had the right of it when I said we should keep that young lady aboard with us. I vow, she'd be a pirate Captain by this time."

"Better than some I've known," said Terrell, nodding his head.

"Aye, and that's a true word," Shoup added emphatically.

Ranald looked at Shoup with interest. He had not thought that anyone but himself could be so emphatic in speaking of Enid Mandeville, and was not sure that he liked it.

Terrell came and put his hand on Ranald's shoulder. "I can't be truly glad you're back, lad, for ye wanted to come no whit," he said. "So let's just say I'm glad ye could come when they had themselves set to hang ye. Come aboard now with the rest of us, come aboard the *Tuscarora*. She'll be a home to ye now, and ye can lay to that."

They sailed out of Topsail Inlet, and eastward by southeastward. The Bermudas would be their objective.

Ranald was eager to see them, perhaps to have adventures.

It would be a voyage of six hundred miles or more, and Ranald had no duties except those of a common seaman. He jumped to orders for shifting sails, and for a while took the tiller to steer them eastward. At evening of the first day, Shoup arrived to take over the steering, and Ranald lingered on the quarterdeck to gaze aft at the setting sun.

"You've worked hard this day, mate," Shoup said to him. "I saw you high up the mast, time and again."

"Aye, to handle the sails," said Ranald.

"Harder duty than charting courses as Sailing Master," Shoup suggested. "And more proper, too, for a tarry sailor than for a schooled and accomplished young gentleman."

"I didn't mind," Ranald said. "Indeed, I liked it."

"But will you like long months of it, in all weathers? Long years?" Shoup glanced at the binnacle, then at Ranald. "Would not Sailing Master be more to your liking and your deserving?"

"But Captain Haws does our navigation now," Ranald reminded.

"And how if he were to navigate no more?" Shoup said, with the ghost of a grin in his beard. "Who could we look to for our navigator but to you?"

Ranald laughed. "Let that come when it comes," he said carelessly. "Captain Haws is better at sailing than I, for he's had long years of experience. He's far older and wiser."

"And closer to death, too," Shoup said.

"What did you say, sir?" Ranald cried out. "Captain Haws to die? Not soon, I hope, for I think him the best man aboard, and the worthiest."

Even as he spoke, Ranald knew his words for truth. He had come to like Haws and to respect him.

"Easy all, shipmate, I did not suggest killing him," said Shoup, smiling again. " 'Twas you who said that he is years older than you. And the older a man is, the sooner he dies, by nature's rule."

"Death is sure to all of us, and life is uncertain," said Ranald. "For all we know, Captain Haws will outlive us both."

"I wonder," Shoup answered.

"Well, the day he dies will be a sad day for this ship and this crew."

Ranald walked down the steps to the main deck. It had been a strange conversation, he thought, and somehow a mysterious one. Then Haws called him down to the big cabin, to discuss the marking of a course on a chart he had spread on the table.

"For the time you're scrubbing decks and reefing sails, but you might have to act Sailing Master again," said Haws. "It might well be that I'd not be able to serve, as I was when we met."

"So Quartermaster Shoup was remarking to me, even now," said Ranald.

"Then Shoup is forethoughted, too. Look you here, we'll approach the Bermudas in two or three days. We may even anchor there, for the officials are none so stern against poor roving seamen as are those fellows who accused you and Dr. Pilbeam. Now, from the Bermudas, how far do you think we might sail to meet a chance Spanish merchant homeward bound? Help me to choose such waters and plan our course to them."

As they worked with compass, rule and dividers, Dr. Pilbeam entered. Captain Haws opened a bottle of Canary and got out a box of biscuits. Pilbeam talked of books and authors, of Jonathan Swift's *Gulliver* and Milton's *Paradise Lost* and the plays of Shakespeare. Ranald enjoyed that talk immensely, and went to bed late that night. He slept soundly in the small cabin he had been allowed to keep.

Cato wakened him in the early morning. Ranald sat up and yawned.

"Breakfast time already?" he asked. "I'm hungry, Cato."

"The men are eating on deck now," said Cato hurriedly. "But go knock on the Captain's door. Say that I'll bring both of you some breakfast, and that I have news for him."

"Why, to be sure," said Ranald. "What news is that?"

"I'll tell the two of you together."

Cato went out. Ranald pulled on his clothes and went to tap with his knuckles at Haws' cabin.

Haws opened the door. He was dressed in shirt and breeches, and sat down to pull on a pair of knee boots as Ranald gave him Cato's message.

"Ha, that hath a mystical sound," said Haws. "Is Cato given to such dramatic behavior?"

"Not Cato, sir. He is usually sober and cautious in all that he says and does."

A knock sounded at the door.

"He is here now, to inform us," said Haws. "Let him in."

Ranald drew the door open. Cato entered, and Ranald shut it again. Cato sat a tray of breakfast dishes upon the table, then straightened and looked thoughtfully at Haws.

"Out with it, Cato," Haws bade him. "What news is it you bring us in this furtive fashion?"

"Very bad news, I fear," said Cato.

"Out with it, I say," urged Haws again, rising to his feet. "Bad news never yet kept well."

"Captain Haws, there's a plan to depose you," Cato said.

"Nonsense!" cried Ranald. "Who would depose him? That would be mutiny."

"Nay, young Blaikie, pirate leaders can be changed at will of their companies," Haws told him. "How do you know of this, Cato?"

" 'Twas Quartermaster Shoup told me, sir," Cato said, in a sudden swift rush. "He drew me aside just now, to sound me out. He said that many of the company are not pleased with how you lead them, and that he's ready to be Captain instead of you."

Ranald stared. "And he wants you to join his party, is that the way of it?"

"Aye, Master Ranald. He said he'd tried to talk to you yesterday. He was ready to promise that you'd be Sailing

Master of his new company. But you had seemed a friend of Captain Haws—too good a friend, it seemed to him."

"Aye, I remember his talk," said Ranald.

"And he remarked that I knew something of navigation," went on Cato. "He told me I could count on the office and a Master's share in prizes."

Haws cleared his throat with a fierce rasp.

"Ha, there was a fat inducement for you, Cato," he said. "But instead of siding with him, you've come to warn me."

"I told him I would think on it, and then I hurried to wake Master Ranald and then come here," replied Cato. "You see, Quartermaster Shoup says he can be Captain by election—the greater part of the crew voting for him. But if that happens, he says, two must die."

"And I'm one of the two, I'll warrant," said Haws, grinning. "He'd never expect me to serve under him. Who's the other?"

"The other," said Cato, "is Master Ranald here. The Quartermaster said that Master Ranald spoke too warmly for you, Captain, that he'd never stand by tamely and see you thrown overside. So both of you are to go overside together."

# *who shall be captain?* | ⚓ **11** ⚓

Listening to Cato's words, Ranald was surprised that he felt no terror, felt nothing but an excited anger. Then he told himself that he had been in too much danger lately to feel terror. Whatever Shoup's threat and however Shoup meant to carry it out, it did not strike Ranald as so desperate as the threat of a shameful death by hanging short days ago.

Whatever Captain Haws might feel, he seemed calm and almost casual.

"Thank you, Cato," he said, as though Cato had done him some routine service. "I know you're telling the truth, because you have a habit of truth-telling. Well, and so Shoup would be Captain, would he, and send Master Blaikie and me to the sharks?"

He smiled broadly, as if it were a joke.

"He'll find it easier thought of than done," he said.

"There are at least three of us together against what force he may bring, Captain," said Ranald. "You and Cato and me."

"Mayhap more than that," said Haws. "Go on out, Cato, as though naught had happened. Say quietly to Harrowby that he is to report to me here. And then to Terrell, that he is to come a moment or so after Harrowby."

Cato nodded and went out. Captain Haws poured himself a cup of coffee from the pot on the tray.

"Will you have some, too?" he invited Ranald. "No? Then go to your cabin and arm yourself. I'll do the same. We may very well have to fight for our lives 'ere much time is gone."

Ranald hurried to his cabin next door. He reached for his sword, then left it hanging there and took instead a stout, serviceable cutlass. Strapping it around his waist, he examined several pistols. They were part of his loot from the two Spanish prizes. He selected a pair, double-barrelled and flintlocked. Carefully he loaded and primed them and stuck them in the belt that held the cutlass. Thus equipped, he returned to Haws' cabin.

Harrowby was there, and as Ranald entered Terrell came down the stairs behind him. Cato followed at Terrell's shoulder.

At once Haws gave Cato a long pistol. "Know you how to use that?" he asked.

"Passing well, sir," said Cato.

"Then go out again, and guard the steps. We don't want to be bottled up in this cabin while we decide what's to be done. Order back any man who approaches. If he will not turn back, shoot him."

"Aye, aye, sir," said Cato, weighing the pistol in a practised hand. He went out and shut the door.

"Shipmates, here's the case, and a troublesome one," Captain Haws said. In the fewest possible words he told Harrowby and Terrell the report Cato had brought. They frowned as they listened.

"Splinter me, but I'd never a hint from Shoup of this," said Terrell when Haws had finished.

"Nor I," said Harrowby. "Nay, why would he tell his plan to Terrell or me? He'd know we were both on your side. No point in sounding us out, as he sounded Master Blaikie."

"I knew you were true friends and stout allies when I sent for you," said Haws. "We're five, then, against Shoup's standing for Captain. Who else may I count on?"

"Dr. Pilbeam," offered Ranald.

"True, he'll stand fast," agreed Harrowby. "And, as I think, most of our old fellowship will prefer Captain Haws. On the other hand, the new men—those we took aboard at Grand Cayman—may well be in Shoup's party."

"That is true," agreed Terrell. "He had the choosing of them, and belike he chose them for this very business. Now, I make our numbers forty-four, and Shoup may well have a majority of the vote, a small majority, by reason of his recruiting."

"I'll wager that big Indian Metoquah will come to us,"

said Harrowby. "And he might swing some of them in our favor."

"Metoquah ventured his life to save Dr. Pilbeam and me when we were in jail," said Ranald. "Had he been part of this conspiracy, he'd have left us there to reduce Captain Haws' number."

Haws had girded himself with a sword, and over his shoulders he slung his scarf with a pistol at each end. He had been loading two more pistols as they talked, and these he shoved, muzzle downward, into the tops of his knee boots.

"Choose any weapons you want here," he told Harrowby and Terrell, and they made haste to pick up cutlasses and pistols. "I take it that Shoup will act according to the articles," went on Haws. "He'll call for a meeting, make his charges against me, and bring it to a vote of all hands. Yet there's no sense in going on deck and calling him to account unless we're ready to defend ourselves."

"I'd best go to the magazine," said Terrell. "Shoup's friends may be arming themselves there."

"Better take Cato with you," said Haws as Terrell opened the door. "If you reach the magazine without question or mishap, he can come back and report. Then we'll step out on deck and tell Shoup to bring his charges."

"We five?" asked Harrowby.

"We five, and whoever may feel Shoup is not apt to make the better Captain," said Haws.

Terrell mounted to the deck, and Cato with him. Harrowby stood halfway up the steps, where he could see out.

"Here comes Cato back," he announced after a few moments. "Then Terrell must have reached his weapon room safely. But I see Shoup on deck, and a group of the men with him. Somebody else must be holding the tiller—Crotty Baker, as I'll warrant. He's a friend to Shoup, and often steers in Shoup's place."

Cato came to the opening above. "Gunner Terrell's in the magazine," he said swiftly, "but they suspect. They're coming along behind me."

"Then up on deck, everyone!" cried Haws.

Harrowby ran up the stairs. Haws mounted after him, and then Ranald.

The day was mild and bright, with only a gentle breeze from the south caught in the sails. Ranald glanced over his shoulder. Sure enough, Shoup was not steering. The tiller was in the hands of short, muscled Crotty Baker, as Harrowby had guessed.

Gathered amidships, between mainmast and foremast, stood fully a dozen men, with Shoup's fierce, bearded face to the fore among them.

"Captain Haws, what is toward?" Shoup challenged roughly. "Why do you and those others come out like that, all of you armed to the teeth?"

"You know the answer to that as well as I, Quartermaster," rejoined Haws, striding past Harrowby. "You're gathering a group of followers to make yourself Captain, and make me food for fishes."

Shoup muttered a curse. He wore a red scarf on his head, and loose shirt and breeches as though for ordinary shipboard duty. But he, too, was heavily armed, with cutlass, knife and pistols at his belt. Several of his companions were similarly equipped with weapons.

"Sir, I do but appeal to the agreement under which we are embodied as a sea-roving company," he said at last, quite calmly. " 'Tis my right, or the right of any of us, to raise questions and make charges, and to call for judgment by majority vote."

"You embarrass me, Shoup," said Haws, who did not appear in the least embarrassed. "Word hath come to me that you seek, not simply to depose me, but to kill me outright. You can't blame me if I make myself ready to fight against that."

Several of the listeners seemed to grin, as though in approval of what Haws said. Shoup may have felt that he had less than complete support, for he glared around him angrily.

"Hark to me, comrades, all of you!" he cried out at the top of his lungs. "I call for an assembly and a decision, here and now!"

Haws seemed to chuckle. "Nay, I'm still Captain until voted out," he said cheerfully. " 'Tis for me to call the assembly, at your request. Where's Bo'sun Harrowby? Pipe all hands hither on deck, Harrowby."

Harrowby took the pipe that hung around his neck by a lanyard and set it to his lips. He blew a shrill, prolonged blast.

"Everybody on deck!" Captain Haws shouted. "How now, Crotty Baker, bring us into the wind and lay to. Then lash that tiller and join us for a council."

The men came at his call, from below decks, from lookout posts high on the masts, from the rails to either side and from the prow. They thickened into a huddle, a little forward of the mainmast. Haws and Shoup walked toward each other, and the men made a ring around them. The two rivals looked into each other's eyes. Baker obediently fetched the ship about, quitted his post and came down to join his companions. Terrell, too, emerged from the hatch that led to the magazine.

"Are all here?" asked Haws. "Every man aboard us? Look to all quarters, is any other craft in view?"

The sea was empty to the horizon, all around.

"Very well, mates," said Haws, "Quartermaster Shoup here says he hath charges to bring against me, and a call to remove me as your Captain." He stared at Shoup again. "Such, friends, is his right. I call on him to speak to his purpose."

Shoup glared back. He held his shoulders square, and his broad hands took hold of his belt near his pistols.

"Speak I shall, and with truth and sense," he announced defiantly. "Gentlemen all and true comrades, what hath our luck been since we felt one ship sink under our feet and came aboard this other? Look back upon it, all of you. We made our way to Grand Cayman, we took on such a crew as a true roving craft should have, and armed ourselves for treasure-seeking. In the months since then, we've taken two small prizes, and got small profit from them. Two prizes, I say, in a space of time when we should have found and taken twenty."

"Aye, rightly said!" growled Crotty Baker, and Shoup grew bolder with that endorsement.

"And what of the two we did take?" he cried out, louder still. "One of them we let go to sail away, after we'd taken money and some cargo—let her go, I say, free and safe, with all her company. The other we sank, but we let her crew take to their boats and escape."

He took his hands from his belt, and flung them out in a full-armed gesture of condemnation.

"To what result?" he shouted. "Those Spaniards returned to their friends, and made report of us. They were able to carry full description of our ship—color, rigging, everything. So that within short days the Spaniards were aware of us, aye, and looking for us to destroy us!"

"Ha, that's even so!" said another voice.

"We had to run for our lives from that great red frigate *Compeador*," Shoup plunged ahead in bitter triumph. "We flew French colors, but the *Compeador* knew that was but a deceit. She chased us into the very shallows off Haiti. Why? Because Captain Reuben Haws chose to let the crews of those ships go free and alive, with their tongues clacking mischief against us."

"What would you have done, Quartermaster?" Pilbeam challenged him. "Would you have killed those helpless men, without mercy?"

"Aye, so I would have done," Shoup flung back swiftly. "And so would Blackbeard have done, and Stede Bonnet, and also James Flint—that's the way of every pirate who knows his business. 'Tis no business for milk-hearted folk, I do agree."

Several exclaimed and nodded vigorously, as though in approval. Shoup seemed to glory in the weight his words were being given.

"You ask me what I would do were I Captain," he said. "I'd have left dead men to tell no tales, in either prize-taking. I'd have kept that first Spanish ship, put a crew of us aboard her, found guns to arm her for action. I'd have found men enough to work and fight her. Two ships instead of one, mates—and, in days to come, more captured ships, more guns and more men, as we found them."

He grinned right and left at the listeners.

"We'd have a whole fleet of rovers," he cried. "We could leave the beggarly, skulking trade of preying upon small merchantmen. We would not flee the big Spanish fleets with their ladings of gold and jewels, we'd seek them out, fight and conquer them. We might well do as Henry Morgan did, seventy years ago—attack harbor towns, capture them, go ashore and reap millions of good gold and silver pieces instead of thousands!"

A sort of cheer went up, here and there, among the pirates.

"But Reuben Haws fears to lead us to such treasures," said Shoup, clenching a fist on high. "So I say, rid ourselves of an unprofitable leader—take one who has the heart and the thought and the method to do these things to make us rich and happy and glorious!"

More of a cheer this time. Ranald asked himself if
Shoup had not won his argument.

"Now," proclaimed Shoup, his hands back to his belt,
"I have said what I have to say. Let someone else
speak."

"Let Captain Haws speak," said Terrell. "He'll have a
word to dry you up, I make no doubt."

Haws laughed easily.

"Nay," he said, "what need for me to plead or argue? I
think that all have heard Tucker Shoup at his most elo-
quent. And each man of you either agrees and backs him,
or disbelieves and mistrusts him. All this, friends, is but
to bring you to a vote. Who among you wishes to name
the man he wants for Captain in my stead?"

"Who but Tucker Shoup?" called out a voice, and
Haws nodded.

"Do you all say that?" inquired Haws gently.

"Not I!" burst out Harrowby at the top of his voice. "I
say, keep Reuben Haws, for the good Captain and seaman he is, the brave man we can trust and follow!"

Another cheer went up at that. Ranald wondered if it
was as loud as the cheer for Shoup.

"And there you have it, mates," said Haws. "One or
other of us it must be. So let me go aft and stand there,
and Shoup may go forward. Let those of you who want
Shoup for Captain, follow him forward. Let any who'd
rather let well enough alone with me, join me where I go
to stand."

The ring parted as Haws turned on his heel and paced
away to the steps that led to the quarterdeck. Shoup

strode the other way, and stopped and turned around at the bow. Some men moved with him.

Ranald swung around and walked after Haws. As he reached Haws' side, Cato came, too. Harrowby and Terrell and Pilbeam followed. Others came. Among them was the huge form of Metoquah, who took his place with Cato and Ranald.

Others were flocking to the bow with Shoup. Less than a minute passed before all except Scratch Walker had made his choice.

Terrell was counting. "Eighteen, nineteen," he said, "twenty, and Cap'n Haws himself makes twenty-one."

"Twenty-two in Shoup's party," said Pilbeam, squinting forward through his spectacles. "One more than us."

"Walker still waits," said Harrowby. "Ahoy, Scratch, which Captain do you want?"

"We have the majority," someone called from the party with Shoup. "Come join us, Scratch."

For a moment Walker lounged amidships. Ranald saw him grin, showing his broken teeth. Then he shrugged, and turned slowly toward the stern. As slowly, he walked to join Haws' supporters. Yells and insults followed him from the group at the bow.

Terrell caught Walker by the hand. "I knew ye'd be with us," he said. "Now it's an even vote, twenty-two against twenty-two."

"I waited to make sure of that," said Walker.

"How, make sure?" Harrowby asked him. "What's your meaning, Scratch?"

"An even vote puts the matter where it belongs," replied Walker. "Betwixt Reuben Haws and Tucker Shoup. Whichever of them is Captain, the other can hardly hope to live and serve under him."

"I see what's in your mind," nodded Terrell.

"Let the two take to their weapons," said Walker. "Who lives to win the fight, him we must all serve and follow."

# *settlement by the sword* | ⚓ **12** ⚓

Again Captain Reuben Haws laughed, as if it were a mild pleasantry.

"Upon my soul, mates, Scratch Walker speaks with some wisdom," he declared. "Often in the past, gentlemen rovers have decided important matters in just that way. The sword is a most final tool of settlement, and there's no appeal from its decision."

Shoup had tramped forward, clear of his clustered followers.

"Ahoy, you there astern!" he cried. "The vote is even. We must vote again, else we have no Captain at all."

"There you are mistaken, Quartermaster," said Haws, also strolling into the open space. "A Captain cannot be deposed save by majority vote, and you've no majority there with you. Therefore I am still Captain."

"Nor do you have a majority," Shoup blustered. "I have an even half of the votes."

Haws nodded his head gravely. "Then perhaps we can make a majority by removing one of the voters. Would not that suffice?"

"How do you mean?" Shoup said.

"Here am I in front of you, giving you leave to try to remove me and my vote," replied Haws. "I will try just as hard to remove you. That should settle things."

Both factions shouted in approval of that. Shoup's eyes resembled chips of pale flint.

"You offer me a challenge," he said.

"Aye, just for the sake of settling our vexing question," Haws agreed. "If one or other of us should cease forever to make claims and charge faults, the matter would be decided. In the interests of our company's welfare, I venture my life against you."

Crotty Baker trotted forward to Shoup's side. "He defies you, Tucker," he said. "Draw and finish him."

Shoup's face split in a fearsome grin. "Aye, why not?"

And his right hand slid to the butt of a pistol.

"Hold hard, Tucker!" warned Terrell hurriedly, and whipped out his own pistol.

"No bullets in this," he snapped. "Try to pistol Cap'n Haws, and I'll slap an ounce of lead into ye. Swords let it be. A single combat and a fair one."

"Aye, aye to that!" cried someone from Shoup's party. "Out blades, both men, and may the better of the two be our Cap'n!"

"And so say I," chimed in Harrowby.

"Yea, yea!" rose a chorus.

"Master Blaikie," said Haws quietly, "do you go stand

by the tiller. Quartermaster Shoup, be kind enough to send one of your friends to keep Blaikie company."

"Go you, Crotty," bade Shoup, and both Ranald and Baker hurried to the steps and mounted the quarter-deck.

"Two more of you up the masts," went on Haws. "You, Walker and Metoquah. Keep your eyes sharp, make sure we have no prying company for the next quarter hour or so."

" 'Twill need no quarter hour to settle this," Shoup sneered.

He swept his cutlass from its sheath with a singing rasp of steel. With his left hand he unbuckled his belt and let it drop, with the pistols and knife, upon the deck. His keen, curved blade whistled as he swung it through the air to try its balance.

Haws unslung his scarf with the pistols attached, and unfastened his own belt. He drew the pistols from his boots, one after the other, and handed the whole armament to Terrell. "Keep my gear for me," he said. Then he rolled the sleeves of his fine white shirt to the elbows, and cleared his own sword from the scabbard.

Standing by the tiller with Baker, Ranald looked and saw that Haws had taken the splendid sword once the property of the *Golondrina's* Captain. Its keen, straight blade shone like silver, and the hilt that curved to protect Haws' knuckles was of brilliant gold and set with jewels. It was a beautiful weapon and must have been worth a small fortune, but to Ranald it looked almost frail when compared to the broad cutlass in Shoup's hand.

Terrell and Harrowby walked into the open space between the two parties, and two of Shoup's friends came out to meet them. They conferred together in whispers, then nodded as though to show agreement. Then Terrell swung around.

"Ahoy, mates, here's how 'twill be done," he said, loudly and emphatically. "Reuben Haws and Tucker Shoup shall meet and fight here in the waist, at the starboard side. The only weapons will be the blades now drawn by the fighters. If anyone tries to get into the fight and make it three instead of two, he will be shot down at once by us who watch." He looked to one group, then the other. "Do ye agree to those terms? Anybody to speak against it? Then silence gives consent."

"Fetch out your man," said one of the other group, and beckoned to Shoup, who again stepped into the open.

Haws, too, advanced, sword in hand. To Ranald, the rivals seemed well matched physically. They were both in the prime of life, Haws perhaps in his late forties, Shoup a few years younger. In height and reach they seemed fairly even. Shoup's muscles were like hard lumps, Haws' arms displayed leaner sinews that seemed like bunches of wire.

None of the watchers stirred or spoke as the two approached each other. Shoup stood firmly on broad, bare feet, his knees slightly bent, the cutlass poised slantingly in front of him with its edge outward. Haws inched closer, his right foot sliding out, his left moving up and setting itself like a pedestal. Haws extended his sword arm. His lean blade quivered, its point seeking an opening.

Shoup's teeth showed white in his shaggy face. He seemed to wait motionlessly for his enemy's advance. Then, as Haws glided within reach, Shoup galvanized into action. His right foot stamped forward as he swept the big cutlass in a powerful cut at Haws' head.

But Haws' blade flashed high in a crosswise parry. It caught that mighty, slashing blow close to the hilt, where the steel was stronger. As he pushed Shoup's cutlass aside, he disengaged and sped a lightning thrust of his own. So close together were they that Haws had only to extend his arm. Shoup had time for but a partial parry, and Haws' point snagged Shoup's shirt at the upper right arm. The group astern raised a joyous cheer to see a fleck of red stain the cloth.

But Shoup was not seriously hurt by that slight wound. He recovered and lunged again, his cutlass gleaming in the sunlight as it fell like a reaping scythe.

The cutlass engaged Haws' interposed blade and struck it aside. Then, lifting his cutlass again, Shoup struck at his enemy's head. It was a blow like that of an axeman seeking to split a block of wood. But Haws brought up his own weapon and deflected it as it fell.

The force of his own sweeping blow nearly put Shoup off his feet. He took two or three scrambling steps to keep his balance, and as he floundered away, Haws flicked him with his blade. It barely touched Shoup's bearded cheek, and blood sprang out there. Bright red it gleamed in the sunlight.

"Finish him, Cap'n!" cried Terrell.

Haws was after Shoup, who wheeled to face him.

There were moments of swift fencing, the blades ringing and rasping against each other. Shoup scowled and strove to land a telling cut, Haws seemed to parry his attacks easily, almost carelessly. His point jabbed close to Shoup's face. As Shoup brought up his cutlass to parry, Haws refused the engagement of blades, dropped his point low and brought it up to threaten Shoup's chest. Shoup had to leap backward to escape. His eyes widened, as though in terror.

"Come, sir, we must keep our audience amused," Haws said genially, moving in again with an advance of his right foot.

Shoup made a hacking blow at Haws' extended sword, but again Haws dipped his point to avoid contact. He extended his arm and Shoup backed hurriedly away from the point that menaced him.

Haws pressed him close, taking the offensive. He plied his slim, keen sword as easily as though it were a reed. Shoup seemed to grow frantic as he defended himself. He panted, as though his efforts had winded him. On the other hand, Haws breathed easily, and wielded his blade with cold, skilful assurance.

Plainly the Captain was far the better swordsman of the two, thought Ranald, and could dispose of Shoup at any moment he wished. Haws even smiled slightly as he effortlessly deflected a hard cut at his head and extended his arm. Shoup retreated to the very bulwark to escape the probing point.

Shoup grimaced as he felt himself trapped there. He sought to send his cutlass edge to Haws' flank. Haws interposed his own blade, which seemed to twine itself around the heavier cutlass. At the same moment, Haws brought his hilt up sharply. The two blades rang out harshly. A yell rose from both parties of onlookers as the cutlass was snatched from Shoup's grasp and went flying, end over end, a dozen feet across the deck.

"He's yours, Cap'n!" Terrell howled.

"Finish him!" urged Harrowby.

Shoup had fled along the bulwark. He sprang up on a gun carriage and clung there, his left hand clutching the top of the high wooden rail. His face had gone white above his beard. But Haws let the smile broaden on his own face, and dropped his point to rest on the deck.

"Nay," he said gently, "I won't attack an unarmed man. Come down from that perch and pick up your weapon."

Shoup's mouth gaped as though to speak. Still holding to the bulwark with his left hand, he darted his right inside his loose shirt. Out he snatched a dark, slim-barrelled pistol. His thumb raked back its hammer.

"You cowardly dog!" Terrell yelled, starting forward.

But even as the pistol came into sight, Haws leaped forward. He thrust high, his whole body extending itself to carry his point to the mark.

His lunge came home at the very center of Shoup's chest. The keen steel drove in and through, to the very hilt. Ranald heard the pistol bark, but already Shoup was toppling backward with the force of that stroke. The bullet sang away into the sky. Shoup slammed down on top of the bulwark, so heavily that the sword was torn from Haws' hand. Up flew Shoup's bare feet, and he went over the side. The water splashed high as he fell into it.

One moment of silence, so profound that Ranald could

hear the soft whisper of wind. Nobody moved, until Terrell rushed to the side, caught the top of the bulwark and hoisted himself up to look over.

"No sign of him!" he cried. "He must have sunk like a stone."

"And good riddance," pronounced Harrowby. He glared at the huddle of Shoup's supporters. "All right, yonder—any more nominations for Captain?"

"Nay," stammered someone. " 'Tis settled, and with a vengeance. Shoup's gone. We're all for Cap'n Haws now."

"Doth any man say nay to that?" Harrowby challenged. "Who'll next set himself up for the post?"

He waited, but nobody spoke.

"Then all's settled," said Terrell. "Naught else to concern us."

"Hold," said Haws. "Tucker Shoup, 'tis true, is no longer one of us. He was our Quartermaster, and his place must be filled."

"Aye, aye, and that's a true word," agreed Terrell. " 'Tis writ in the articles that the Cap'n names his choice for any post, and the crew votes yea or nay."

"Even so," Haws nodded. "And, mates, I have a name to put before you. The man's up yonder on the quarter-deck."

All looked that way. Crotty Baker, beside the tiller, smiled joyfully.

"Shoup himself thought well of this man's qualities," went on Haws. "He can handle a ship as well as the best. He is brave, and of good wit and presence."

Baker was inflating his chest.

"And, too, he has proven his worth and fairness," Haws elaborated. "He can be trusted as yourselves when he divides prize takings."

"Ha, Captain Haws, I do thank you!" Baker cried.

"As Quartermaster," said Haws, "I nominate—Ranald Blaikie."

A gasp went up from Baker.

"Ranald Blaikie?" he repeated. "Why, sir, he's but a lad."

"And growing older with every moment he breathes," flung back Harrowby. "Look you, mates, he played the man's part when he navigated us from the North Carolina coasts to Grand Cayman, and played the man's part again when he was taken prisoner with Dr. Pilbeam at Edenton. Egad, Blaikie hath my vote for Quartermaster."

"And mine," said Terrell.

"Aye, aye!" others shouted.

"Then who votes nay?" called out Haws. He waited a moment, looking here and there.

"I say he's but a boy," said Baker again, unhappily. "How could salty old seamen take orders from him?"

"Who else against Blaikie?" Haws asked.

Two or three of the party that had supported Shoup muttered.

"It doth not sound like a majority against," Haws said. "Then I declare him elected to those duties and those shares in prizes that fall to Quartermaster. Respect him in his post, you who will stay aboard."

"Stay aboard, sir?" quavered Crotty Baker. "You don't mean you'll fling us overboard, like Tucker Shoup?"

"Nay," laughed Haws. "I but say that you and any others who don't want to stay with this company will be set ashore among friends."

And he looked to where Ranald stood. "Quartermaster Blaikie," he said briskly, "we won't sail on to the Bermudas, after all. Steer us a course northwest by west, for Topsail Inlet, where we'll leave any who aren't contented."

"Aloft, lads, to shift sail!" cried Harrowby.

Ranald freed the tiller from its lashings and began to bring the ship round upon the course ordered by Haws.

## *the chase* ⚓**13**⚓

For a day and a night and most of the next morning, they returned westward. Ranald, as Quartermaster, kept the tiller most of each day. Walker relieved him from time to time, and Cato steered part of the night. By the time they entered Topsail Inlet and anchored off the beach at Tomlinson's, four of Shoup's erstwhile supporters asked to be set ashore. Crotty Baker pleaded to stay with the *Tuscarora*, but Haws shook his head.

"You mistrust and challenge Quartermaster Blaikie," said Haws. "Ashore with you and your possessions. Belike another rover will put in for recruits 'ere long."

The crew spent that night ashore, merry with what refreshment Tomlinson could provide. At dawn the next day, the *Tuscarora* weighed anchor and cleared Topsail Inlet.

"Sail ho!" yelled the lookout up the foremast. "Off the starboard bow to southward!"

Ranald, at the tiller, looked in that direction. So did Haws, at the rail of the quarterdeck.

A ship was there, perhaps five miles distant. Her square sails were set and she was making swift way.

"Northeast, and quick's the word!" ordered Haws. "Yonder may be a ship of war, and that tag of color may be the British flag."

Ranald turned the *Tuscarora* in the new direction. Harrowby shouted for men to adjust the sail. Haws set his spyglass to his eye and manipulated its sliding sections.

"British she is," he said after a moment. "Seems to have guns—two at her bow, anyway. We won't stop to gossip with her. Ahoy, Harrowby, clap on more sail!"

It was like the chase by the *Compeador,* thought Ranald, his eye on the compass in the binnacle. They had to flee a stronger pursuer, try to run away or seek shelter.

"Captain," he ventured, "we're seventy-five miles almost due southwest of Cape Lookout, and another twenty-five miles or so beyond there will fetch us to Stryker's Inlet. You'll remember that for a shallow way through the Outer Banks. If we can run ahead of that ship for a hundred miles, we can get through into Pamlico Sound beyond. A larger vessel than ours can never follow."

"Well thought of," Haws applauded. "We've a brisk wind astern, we're lately cleared of weed, and we run light. Seamanship will fetch us to that refuge, but how can we come out again?"

"If she waits in the bay there at Stryker's, we can sail a

thought northward within, and there's that other inlet where we might win through with some care," said Ranald. "Or if she coasts outside the banks to find another way through, we can put about and return through Stryker's when she's gone."

"We can do it," said Haws, looking at the wind-crowded sails. "I like not to run from a British ship, but I'd like less to fight one." He looked at his watch. "Seven o'clock. How soon, think you, can we be at Stryker's Inlet?"

"At this rate, two o'clock," estimated Ranald.

"Good, good. We'll have a rising tide then, to see us safely through."

Ranald glanced astern. The pursuing ship was making swift way, too. Ranald took her for a three-master, big, but tall and trim, and she was crowding on all her canvas. Even at that distance, it was evident that studding sails were out on both sides of the working sails at the masts.

Terrell came up from the main deck, with several gunners. Metoquah was one. Terrell craned his neck at the following ship.

"Doth she recognize us for rovers, Cap'n, like that big Spaniard, the *Compeador*?" he asked.

"I doubt it," Haws replied. "But she sees us making all haste to distance her, and she's suspicious. Master Blaikie here suggests we run swiftly up to Stryker's Inlet. Our friend astern there may gain on us, but not enough to hull us as did the *Compeador* last April."

"We'll make ready, just in case," said Terrell, as his

gunners cleared the stern swivel for action. Metoquah held the linstock, but did not light the match. All hands on the quarterdeck watched the British ship astern. Even Ranald glanced from time to time at it as he steered.

She gained, very slowly. To some degree, it was like the chase they had led the *Compeador* west of Haiti.

Harrowby had assigned seamen to the rigging overhead and to posts on deck near the lines that governed action of the sails. Now he, too, mounted the quarterdeck. He adjusted his own spyglass to look at the vessel coming after them.

"A frigate, I call her," he said. "Full twenty guns aboard her."

"Say rather twenty-four," was Terrell's expert judgment. "Most, if not all, firing at longer range and with heavier shot than our biggest and best. Belike she thinks we're a Spaniard. By now she can make out some of our guns, so she knows we're armed for fighting."

"If she catches us, 'twill go as hard with us as with any Spaniards," commented Harrowby.

"But she won't catch us," said Haws confidently. "Blaikie steers like the prince of helmsmen, uses every ounce of wind."

"I know these waters, sir," said Ranald, his eye on the compass. "As our course lies, we head straight as an arrow for Cape Lookout. From there, we may lie close in to the banks for Stryker's. It may be that yonder frigate is less sure of how to follow us."

They fairly scudded along. No log was overside, but Ranald estimated their speed at a good fourteen knots. The *Tuscarora* was built for swiftness, and her square topsails gave her power and steadiness. She seemed to soar like a bird.

Haws went below to study his charts, then reappeared on the quarterdeck. He opened his mouth to give an order, but before he spoke he glanced at the compass.

"Faith, but you're on the course I charted ere I can tell you what it is!" he exclaimed.

"I know these waters," said Ranald again.

"You steer by inspiration."

"Never by inspiration, only by having steered up to Lookout many times 'ere this."

Haws gazed backward at the frigate. "We hold our own, or almost, with yonder ship so eager to come up with us. But I want her closer than that when we come to our inlet. See, she fires."

Ranald turned around. He saw a distant dab of murk, the smoke of a cannon. "How can she hope to reach us?" he asked.

"That's but her signal for us to heave to," Haws said. "When we refuse, she'll be the more eager to catch up and learn why."

"And when she does?" Ranald suggested.

"She never will, if we have but a crumb of rover's luck," Haws said confidently.

The pirates kept their posts, ready to jump at any command of Haws or Harrowby, but they seemed to share their Captain's assurance. They smiled and chatted, and a group of them raised a snatch of their favorite song:

> "The people, they will flock
> Unto Execution Dock . . . "

Hardly a happy omen, reflected Ranald, his hand on the tiller and his eye now on the compass, now on the crowded sails, now on the sea ahead. He, at least, saw no fun in the prospect of dangling aloft to entertain a curious crowd. As he steered, he thought back upon his adventures of the past few months.

Walker took the tiller for a while. Ranald went to the galley, where Cato served him with coffee and a slice of hot bread.

"We run from danger again, Master Ranald," said Cato, pouring his own cup of coffee. " 'Tisn't my notion of bold, terrible pirates, always on the run like this."

"Well that we can show our heels," replied Ranald. "Cato, how if we set you ashore when we dodge through Stryker's Inlet? You, at least, aren't marked blackly in the books of the law. Once on land, and money in your pocket, you could win home and tell our tale."

"Never think of sending me from you," Cato said fiercely. "I won't head home till you can head home, too."

"I feared you'd say that," said Ranald.

"You knew I'd say that," rejoined Cato, and smiled.

Ranald went on deck again. He watched the sails, taut in the wind, gazed here and there across the sea. The morning went on toward noon, and again Ranald took the tiller.

The gun crew lounged at the stern swivel, while Terrell peered through Harrowby's glass at the frigate that kept after them so stubbornly. She had drawn closer.

"Nobody aboard us ever saw that craft, or heard tell of one like her," said Terrell. "She's new in these waters, armed to fight Spaniards or slay pirates. There may be more like her these days, here and there off these coasts."

"How if another such came in sight ahead?" suggested Harrowby.

"Then 'twould be up with us," said Terrell cheerfully. "Up aloft, to dangle from our own yardarms, every mother's son."

There again was the rough joke about the end in store if they were caught, by the English or the Spanish. Ranald wished that he had never seen these pirates, that he had never bargained so shrewdly for lives they would have spared anyway, that he was safe somewhere else, anywhere else, than where he was.

Noon came and passed. The watch on the foremast raised a cry of "Land ho!", and Ranald knew it was Cape Lookout, ahead and somewhat to port. He shifted course slightly to take them straight at it.

Behind them, the frigate had gained again. She fired another gun, audible this time, to order them to heave to. Terrell laughed.

"Let them waste powder!" he cried. "We're safe, or nearly. But don't run us aground, mate."

"I won't," said Ranald.

He fetched them around the Cape, so snugly that they could see the stunted trees ashore. The course now lay a point more to westward. The *Tuscarora* skimmed along in sight of the Outer Banks.

Ranald remembered how he had sailed this same route in the shallop with Dr. Pilbeam and Cato and Metoquah.

That had been little more than a week ago. He had made the journey in high hopes of a joyous return home. Today he travelled the same way, the same waters, but with no such hope.

Hope indeed, he mused bitterly as he steered them along the great line of beach. What hope was there for one who followed piracy, whether of his own wish or will or from necessity as in his own case? His mates aboard had remarked again and again that the day of the pirate was in its late afternoon. No longer could a fearsome chief of sea-rovers, like Henry Morgan, summon a fleet of ships manned by daring followers to reap fortunes and strike terror throughout the seven seas. No longer might cunning freeboaters like Blackbeard contrive friendships with high officials to keep themselves safe and easy between plundering voyages. Pirates were few these days. They sought only small, helpless quarry. When a ship of any armament challenged them, they must run, as the *Tuscarora* ran now.

The frigate rounded the Cape, only two miles astern. It came on with every hand's breadth of canvas its tall masts could carry.

"How far now to Stryker's Inlet?" Harrowby asked Ranald.

"We pass Drum Inlet twenty-five miles above Cape Lookout," Ranald made answer. "Five miles above Drum is Stryker's."

Haws looked at his watch. "By two, I judge, we'll be there," he said. "The tide will be flowing, plenty of water to take us through. How about our friend astern? Can a tall frigate, drawing twelve or fourteen feet, follow us there into Pamlico Sound?"

"At tide's rise, barely," said Ranald. "And not swiftly in any case, even if the men aboard know Stryker's Inlet well. If they win through, we can sail the other side a very short space, and come into open sea again beyond."

"We saw that way as we came through Stryker's, our first day aboard this ship," put in Harrowby. "How is it called, mate?"

" 'Tis so small and so little used, I don't think it hath a name," Ranald replied. "Yet I've often gone through, and I can fetch us out there, with the water we'll have."

"Friends, our luck joined us when Blaikie signed our articles," declared Haws. "We go in at Stryker's. If the frigate creeps in after us, we sail out at that other place. Then away east for the Bermudas, over the horizon ere they know we're gone."

Even Ranald felt cheered by this comradely praise.

Up and up they went, and past Drum Inlet. Not many minutes later, the baylike basin where Stryker's Inlet flowed came in view. It was perhaps a third of a mile from south to north, dishing inward, with trees all around. At its northern end rose a high, spurlike tip, almost like a cliff of sand, matted with grass and brush.

"Hold hard," cautioned Haws. "Let yonder zealous hanger on our heels come close enough to see us put in as for a harbor. Then take us through."

It was done. Sails were shifted, the *Tuscarora* slackened speed. On came the frigate, within a mile now, within less than a mile. Again a gun boomed, a cannon ball skipped along the waves.

"Now, in with her!" shouted Haws.

Ranald shifted the tiller strongly, Harrowby called for a trim of the sails. The *Tuscarora* headed into the basin and straight for the inlet. As she slid smoothly between the narrowed banks toward the sound on the far side, the frigate gained the outer reach of the basin. A thunder of a cannon, a shot moaned in the air and struck the sand to starboard.

Terrell laughed aloud, and Metoquah smiled grimly. Ranald saw that smile, then gave all his attention to fetching them through. Carefully he steered the length of the strait until he saw the waters widen at the inner mouth of the inlet. Out he brought the *Tuscarora* and shifted the tiller to curve them northward and seek the shelter of the long, hummocky shore.

"Zookers, mates, she's laying to out yonder," reported Harrowby. "She studies how to squeeze after us. 'Tis like a hound at a hare's burrow."

"Easy as she goes," commanded Haws. "Stay in view to draw her. I want her to worry in after us, and if she grounds on the way, so much the better. If she grounds not, 'twill yet be a tedious matter for her to clear. Then we can head up and out and fling her a goodbye kiss—"

A loud boom of a cannon. Then another, and another.

"What's that?" Haws cried. "Not the British frigate, she is not firing. Who else, then?"

And more guns thundered, in terrible chorus.

# rovers to the rescue ⚓14⚓

The *Tuscarora* had hove to, spilling the wind from her sails. Ranald, at the tiller, could lean back and see along the inlet. On the far side of the passage, the British craft was coming about. At a distance beyond her showed the sails of a mighty ship, among great dark clouds of powder smoke.

Haws sprang to the after rail and leaned above it to see. He, too, stared along the inlet.

"Red, I see a red hull!" he cried. "Upon my soul, mates, that's the *Compeador* herself—she's popped up from nowhere to open fire!"

As he spoke, two tiers of flashes sprang out along the side of the *Compeador*. The frigate seemed to shudder. She was being hit.

Haws faced around. Terrell and his gunners looked at him, eyes wide. Harrowby came rushing along the quarterdeck.

"The *Compeador?*" he echoed. "Nay, how could she be here with nobody aware?"

More firing. The frigate was returning that broadside.

"See to that Britisher, she dares not try the inlet after us," said Haws. "She turns to fight—aye, and that with British pluck."

"Pluck," Terrell said after him, "and twenty-four guns, I make it, against full forty-eight." They listened to a new thunder of shots. "If she comes not after us," said Terrell, "her only way out is under the very cannon of the *Compeador.* What chance hath she?"

"I can say how the *Compeador* hid," offered Ranald. "Did you mark that height of ground at the northern end of the basin? She could lurk there unseen, and show herself only to cut off her prey from the sea."

Haws shot a glance upward at the sails. "Set us to make way north for that other passage," he cried, and men sped to obey. "How far must we go, Blaikie?"

"Minutes only," said Ranald.

Terrell had been watching the scowl on Haws' face. "Cap'n," he said slowly, "I know what ye're thinking just now."

"Do you so?" snapped Haws, spinning on a heel and looking at Terrell.

"Aye, sir, I read ye like fair print," said Terrell, his voice bold. "Ye come of English blood—and so do I." Terrell's own hard face drew into bitter lines. "And so do those men who fight out there, against those heavy Spanish odds."

"I'm English born, too," said Harrowby.

"And I," added a gunner, leaning on his sponge staff.

Haws darted a look at them, all around him. "Are you trying to say you'd strike a blow on the English side?"

"I would, if I could," Ranald told him at once.

"But how could we?" demanded another gunner. "That *Compeador's* twice the size and metal of the frigate, and four times any strength we have."

"Aye, but if we could!" Haws cried out, shaking his fists at the sky. "If we could steal upon the *Compeador*—"

" 'Twould be like a dog stealing upon a bear," said Harrowby.

"But a true fighting dog," argued Terrell, "upon a bear that dreamed not the dog was even at hand."

"I'm for fighting," shouted a gunner with a gray beard. "Isn't one gentleman of fortune, who knows his blade and his gun, worth three Spaniards?"

"True you speak, we're their betters at close quarters or far!" applauded the man next to him.

A little cheer went up from the group on the quarterdeck. Men at other stations looked that way.

"Blaikie, you say we have minutes ere we make that upper passage," said Haws. "Harrowby, pipe all hands here for a council."

Harrowby's pipe shrilled, even as more cannon spoke from the far side of the bank. The seamen hurried from their posts on deck or slid down ropes from aloft, to gather at the break of the quarterdeck. Haws stepped forward to confront them.

"Lads," he said earnestly, "is any one of you afraid of a good fight and a hard one? If that's your case, then speak now, and we'll set you ashore this instant."

He paused, waiting. Nobody made a sound.

"Last spring we were shot to pieces, by that Spanish warship *Compeador*," Haws went on. "Early in August, we were fain to run before her. Now she's back, within close reach, and we up here on the quarterdeck are of a mind to try for revenge. Doth any other man aboard think like that?"

Still nobody spoke. The men looked blank.

"We're but a little clam shell against a shark of the sea," said Haws, his voice rising. "But we've stout hearts and true eyes and strong hands aboard us. And we're not alone—there's that British frigate—"

A great crashing peal of gunfire sounded.

"Hark, mates!" cried Haws, bending to look into the faces before him. "Out there she makes a fight of it. She, too, is small against the *Compeador*, but she'll win or die!"

"And hurrah for her!" yelled a big seaman.

"And a curse on that raiding Spaniard!" roared another. "I'm with ye, Cap'n Haws!"

"We'll slip up on her while she hath her hands full with the frigate," said Haws, as though he already knew how to do it. "We can come to grips with her, and see which men are the better. Who says no to battle? Speak and go ashore, or come on with the rest of us!"

A chorus of approving yells rang out.

"Fight's the word!" one man cried. "Lead us!"

Ranald, steering, listened in utter amazement. This handful of men, in a schooner dwarfed by the giant *Compeador* and heavily outclassed in numbers and guns, voted joyously for battle. Nobody even seemed to stop to think.

" 'Tis Captain Haws they trust," said Harrowby beside Ranald, as though he understood Ranald's wonder. "Let him say we can win and they're sure that we've half won already."

Haws sprang down upon the main deck and gave emphatic orders to Walker, who raced away on an errand.

"Cato," said Haws, "fetch a tub of grog on deck, and let all hands dip from it. Dr. Pilbeam, you can spread canvas here next the cabin steps for wounded to lie on. You can have the cabins—any or all of them—for surgery. Gunner Terrell!"

"Aye, aye, sir," and Terrell leaped down to him.

"Man that forward swivel with your best gunners."

"I'll want Metoquah—" Terrell began.

"No, Metoquah's for another duty. Pick any but him." Haws looked up to the quarterdeck. "How far are we from that way through, Blaikie?"

"A minute or so this side of it, Captain," Ranald made reply. " 'Twill be slow passing the inlet itself."

The guns growled out of sight. Cato was serving out grog on deck. Walker came toward Haws, dragging a great tow sack that seemed to hold blocks of wood. On his shoulder he carried two heavy mallets.

"Make the longboat ready to cast off," Haws directed

Walker. "Metoquah goes with you. Choose six who can row swiftly and strongly. You're ready for what's toward?"

"Aye, sir, and happy to do it," replied Walker, with a grin. "Here, you and you and you—yes, and you big fellow, and you two—stand by to launch and handle the oars."

Ranald wondered what the boat would do, but then gave all his attention to his steering. The narrow strait appeared ahead. Ranald pushed the tiller hard to port and guided the *Tuscarora* in.

The tide was well up, he noted thankfully, but it still would be a tricky maneuver. Never had he attempted that cramped passage with a craft anywhere near the size of the *Tuscarora*.

Terrell had assembled four gunners at the long bow swivel and set them to clearing it. Then he beckoned two more men and they plunged down the hatch to fetch up armloads of muskets and pistols, bundles of cutlasses. Seamen seized the weapons. At Haws' order, two parties of them scrambled up the rigging to the mastheads, carrying guns and powder horns and bullet pouches. Every man seemed to know what would be expected of him.

Again and again the guns spoke from the far side of the banks. Haws mounted swiftly to the quarterdeck, just as Ranald nosed the *Tuscarora* between the two shores of the inlet.

"Easy as she goes," Haws cautioned him. "If we run aground now, we're out of it, and helpless prey to whichever ship wins that loud battle. Now, sir, when we clear to east of here, can you fetch us along out of sight of the *Compeador?*"

"I think so, if we lie in close," Ranald said. "But we'll go at a slow pace. We must luff around and sail almost into the wind."

"At the quarters I hope to bring us to, slowly is swift enough." Haws looked up the mainmast. "Ahoy, there!" he called to the two parties aloft. "Are you ready?"

"Aye, aye, sir," came back the cheerful reply.

"Wait for the bow swivel to fire first, and then do your duty." Haws beckoned Harrowby. "Up with the British flag."

"I have it here." Harrowby unfolded a Union Jack, made it fast to the halyard, and drew it up to the main peak.

In gingerly fashion, Ranald piloted the ship through the channel. So fixed was his attention upon his steering that he barely heard the continuous voices of the cannon. He strained his ears for any sound of scraping bottom, but none came. The *Tuscarora* slid along smoothly. Up ahead, he saw the waters opening before him. With breathless attention, Ranald fetched his ship through and into the sea.

"Well done, youngster," Haws praised him. "Hard aport now, and fetch us along to that height above the mouth of Stryker's Inlet." He stepped to the edge of the quarterdeck. "Walker, is the longboat ready? Then launch her, but keep her tied up until I give the order."

Walker had flung his sack of wooden blocks and the

two mallets into the bottom of the boat. The others of his crew opened the port hatch through the bulwark and slid the boat down and into the sea, hopping into it as it struck water and righted itself. The rowers stood with oars pointing upward, every man armed with a belt full of weapons. Walker took steering position at the tiller. Metoquah, at the bow, poised a boarding axe above the painter that connected the boat to the *Tuscarora.*

To Ranald, it seemed that every man except himself knew what would happen, what to do. Bunched at the bow swivel stood Terrell's gunners, stripped to the waist and waiting tensely. Terrell poised a linstock. Ranald saw him blow on the lighted match it held. The two parties up the masts held muskets at the ready. Pilbeam stood beside the cabin stairs, a length of canvas spread out and a medicine chest open. Metoquah and Walker and the others in the longboat also seemed to await a moment of planned action. Half a dozen other seamen were ranged along the starboard bulwark, pistols and cutlasses at their sides, muskets in their hands.

Cato mounted the quarterdeck and held out a belt with Ranald's sword attached.

"We aren't pirates now," he said. "We're just fighting seamen."

Ranald's hands were busy with the tiller, and Cato buckled the sword belt for him and shoved two pistols into it. Up ahead the height that marked the opening of the Stryker's Inlet estuary approached. The noise of the guns was so tremendous now, it seemed to make the sky quiver.

"Longboat away!" cried Haws above the racket.

Metoquah brought down his axe and severed the painter. He shoved with all his might against the ship's side to send the longboat sliding clear. The six rowers instantly set the oars in the locks and pulled powerfully to send their craft ahead of the creeping *Tuscarora*. Walker seized the tiller and guided them.

So swiftly did they row that they drew well ahead and to port. Metoquah, at the bow, stood erect with feet powerfully braced. He seemed to gaze past the height of land and see something. Turning, he made a great gesture with both arms. Walker understood what he meant, and beckoned toward the ship.

"Bravo!" shouted Haws. "Bring us around and at them!"

Steering so close to shore that he almost shaved it, Ranald tried to think of all he had heard about sea fighting. Old sailors had always talked of getting the weather gauge. That meant, to be to windward of the enemy, and surely the *Compeador* could hardly be more to windward than now. What then? Ranald did not even know how to ask.

He steered them around the big bluff to starboard, and into view of the battle below.

*the sea fight* ⚓ **15** ⚓

Almost straight ahead was the great red Spanish ship, three-quarters hidden in a cloud of dark powder smoke. She lay headed southward as though to command the wide mouth of the inlet's estuary, and her stern was no more than a cable's length from the prow of the *Tuscarora*. Well forward of the *Tuscarora* sped the longboat, ripping through the water under the frantic efforts of the oarsmen. And deep within the estuary, the British frigate was visible.

She, too, was masked in smoke, but less heavily than the *Compeador*. Ranald could see that her foremast was down, as though felled by shots. But she had sail on the other two masts, and was coming about as though to present her broadside to the *Compeador,* at perhaps three hundred yards' range.

Even as Ranald headed the *Tuscarora* straight for the *Compeador's* stern, the smoke about the great ship lifted somewhat. Ranald made out the fluttering flag of Spain and saw, too, the lines of the ship herself. She had three towering masts, from which all canvas had been stripped except jibs and skysails, the rig for fighting. Both fore and aft she was built high. Her stern showed two pairs of gunports, one pair above the other. Ranald thought he saw the flash of metal inside them.

With every moment, the distance lessened. The longboat, out ahead, strained closer to that huge vessel. The *Tuscarora* neared, yard by yard. The British vessel within the basin completed her coming about. From her side gushed new fire and smoke, a whole bank of guns discharged at once.

Some of those shots struck the *Compeador,* for she quivered in the water. At the same instant, a gun spoke from one of the stern ports. But the shock had disturbed its aim, and the ball went splashing into the sea, wide of the longboat.

"Hold our nose straight at that Spaniard," Haws directed Ranald. "We're opening on her."

At the bow, Terrell bent his knees and looked along the barrel of the swivel, as though to sight it. Then he stepped clear of the breach and dipped his linstock, setting match to the touch hole.

The gun barked and leaped. A joyous cheer went up from the crew that served it, for the ball slammed straight at the *Compeador's* stern. It struck the point between the upper and lower pairs of gunports. Big ragged scraps of wood flew in the air like leaves in the wind, and a splintering crash sounded.

"Clap to the target, by heaven!" exulted Haws. "Keep us at her, Blaikie. You must help Terrell strike her again."

The gunners worked like demons, swiftly sponging the piece and ramming home another charge. Another gun spoke from a port on the *Compeador's* stern, and its ball ripped through the *Tuscarora's* mainsail. Terrell shifted his piece and stooped to sight along it. They were close now, very close. The longboat had come almost under the outer bulge of the stern. Again Terrell applied his match, again the brass gun spoke, and again the shot went smashingly home among those ports.

Next instant, the men in the *Tuscarora's* tops opened fire with muskets. Their shots rattled like pebbles in a shaken gourd. Ranald spared them a look. He saw that only two men of each group fired, while their comrades passed loaded guns to them and rammed fresh charges into those emptied and handed them back. Plainly the four finest shots were slapping lead in at those stern ports, striking down the Spanish gunners or driving them from their positions.

"A point, just a point to port," Haws ordered Ranald. "Bring us to her—put us in alongside, right up against her!"

With that he sprang down from the quarterdeck. He had drawn his sword, and flourished it as he shouted to the men on the main deck. They leaped upon the gun carriages, each levelling a musket above the railing.

The longboat, close up against the *Compeador,* now made its errand clear. The oarsmen struck grappling irons into the wood of the Spanish ship to hold their boat snug. Metoquah and Walker stood up, and Walker shook big wooden wedges out of the bag. Metoquah set one between the *Compeador's* rudder and stern post, then drove it in with mighty blows of a mallet. Walker inserted another and used his own mallet. The wedges jammed the rudder, the *Compeador* could not steer.

Guns went off again, from both the warships. The smoke billowed. Ranald's nostrils tingled with it as he steered the *Tuscarora* into the cloudy murk. The *Compeador* loomed like a red castle. Ranald sent his ship's prow along the *Compeador's* flank, like a hound nosing a stag. The two sides grated together, with a shock that almost threw Ranald from his feet.

The pirates at the rail shoved muskets in at a row of gunports and fired. The *Tuscarora's* topmen fired, too, all of them together this time, down at the Spaniards on the decks below. Then the men with Haws hurled grappling irons high and over the side of the *Compeador* and went swarming up after them, cutlasses in their mouths and pistols in their hands. Terrell's gunners left their piece and rushed to join the boarding party.

Yells and gunshots rang out aboard the *Compeador*. Ranald quitted the tiller, rushed to the rail and ran along it, like a cat along the top of a fence. The line of a grappling hook dangled near. Ranald seized it and swung himself up and into the waist of the red ship, upon the main deck between the high housings at prow and poop.

That main deck was strewn with bodies. Some of them writhed or struggled, others lay slack and silent. Here

and there were guns of the upper batteries, slewed from
their ports or knocked from their carriages by the im-
pacts of heavy shot. A bitter hand-to-hand fight was
waged there by the pirates against the Spanish crew.

Haws was already in the thick of it. He thrust at a man
who wielded a pike, cleared his blade as his foe went
down, and sprang across the falling body to attack another. The pirates were far outnumbered, yet they raged
and slashed at their enemies on all sides.

As Ranald gained the main deck, the parties up the
masts of the *Tuscarora* slid swiftly down the rigging and
aboard the *Compeador*. They had dropped their muskets
as they came down. Rushing at the Spaniards, they fired
pistols at close range, then drew cutlasses.

Close to Ranald a voice roared in Spanish. A glaring
man in a splendid coat and cocked hat was charging. He
lifted a long, gleaming blade on high. Ranald sprang
back, drawing his own sword. But before he could en-
gage his assailant, a dark arm thrust over his shoulder
from behind and fired a pistol. The swordsman fell in a
heap at Ranald's feet.

"That finished him," said Cato's voice at Ranald's ear.

"You may have saved my life," was all that Ranald had
time to say as, side by side, they rushed toward the
fight.

So furiously and skilfully did the pirates use cutlass
and pistol that the superior numbers of Spaniards seemed
actually to falter before them. Ranald tried to close with
one Spaniard, but the fellow turned and fled before him
in dismay. Down from the high deck Walker, Metoquah

and others of the longboat party were dropping. Somehow they had scaled that great height of the poop, and they must have overcome the survivors upon it. Metoquah strode into the thick of the hottest fighting. His great boarding axe rose and fell.

Ranald found himself face to face with a pikeman. A clublike stroke of the Spaniard's big weapon broke Ranald's sword off, close to the hilt, and Ranald clutched the haft of the pike with both hands. Back and forth they struggled until Ranald, with a desperate twist and tug, wrenched the pike from the other's hands. Tipped off balance, the Spaniard fell backward and down an open hatch.

"Look out!" cried Cato.

Ranald wheeled just as another Spanish officer came at him with thrusting blade. The quarters were too close for a stab with the pike, and Ranald whipped the butt around. He rapped the officer's head smartly, knocking his hat off. Down went his opponent, arms and legs sprawling. Ranald stooped and snatched the sword from his hand.

As he did so, a deep-chorused shout rang from the starboard rail of the *Compeador*.

Over that rail a bowsprit was suddenly thrust, and men came pouring aboard. Ranald saw the red coats of British marines, and heard orders shouted in English. The new party fired a volley, and down went more Spaniards. There was a rush. The survivors of the *Compeador* were thrown into disorder, jammed between the pirates and the British marines. There were loud yells in Spanish for mercy. Spanish hands flung down their weapons and reached aloft.

"We've won!" Ranald heard Haws' joyous cry. "Don't kill any more of them, mates. Herd them together."

Across the deck tramped a British officer. He looked to be in his middle fifties, lean and raw-boned, with a hard-jawed face. His gray hair was tousled, his brow bound in a scrap of cloth. The right sleeve of his gold-laced coat had been ripped from cuff to shoulder. In one hand he carried a sword, in the other a pistol that still smoked.

"What, have they yielded so quickly?" he asked. "Who's friend here, and who's foe? What ship is that, the one that came to our help in such good time?"

As the marines and the pirates worked together to round up the cowed, submissive Spaniards, Haws lowered the point of his own bloody sword to the deck.

"I'm Captain Reuben Haws, sir," he said, "and these men are of my company aboard the *Tuscarora*."

The British officer looked him up and down. "Captain Warrick Utterson, His Majesty's frigate *Jason*," he introduced himself gruffly. "You got us out of a tight scrape, sir. When we can be sure of our victory and have time, I'll be proud and happy to shake your hand."

By now the Spaniards were shoved into a close huddle. On one side stood the pirates, on the other the British, all with ready cutlasses and guns. Ranald told himself that, even in defeat, the Spaniards outnumbered the British. More than a hundred must have been struck down by the frigate's bombardment and by the boarding parties, but fully another hundred survived.

"I don't know how you wedged their rudder, but it made them powerless to steer and they couldn't shoot at us as we came to close quarters," went on Utterson. "I'll hear the story of how you did it with interest. Now, who's their Captain?"

Haws turned to the prisoners and repeated the question in Spanish. One of the men pointed mournfully at a limp, motionless figure lying face down on the deck.

"That's the one Cato pistolled," said Ranald.

"Is it, in sooth?" said Haws. "When he fell, the fight started to drain out of these others. Then who is the ranking officer left alive?"

Another fallen Spaniard rose weakly to one knee. It was the one Ranald had knocked down with the butt of the pike.

"I am Lieutenant del Avalenada," he said thickly, in broken English. "My congratulations, señores. Somehow you have won a great victory."

"Give up your sword, sir," Captain Utterson ordered him.

The Spanish Lieutenant stood erect, then gazed blankly around. "My sword?" he said. "But it is gone."

"I have it here," said Ranald, offering it to Utterson.

"Nay, young sir," and Utterson waved it away. "You seem to have taken it in fair fight. 'Tis yours. Let's declare this Spanish warship surrendered."

A marine was bringing down the flag. Parties from the two victorious ships ranged here and there. A marine sergeant saluted Utterson and reported that the four guns at the *Compeador's* stern ports had been disabled by the sure shots landed among them. Spanish gunners were fetched up from the deck below. Terrell supervised the carrying of several wounded pirates back aboard the *Tuscarora.*

"Well, sir," said Utterson to Haws, "plain to see that your ship is no ship of war."

"Say you so, Captain?" smiled Haws. "After what we've done here? Surprising this ship, attacking her with only a tithe of her power—and having the battle won ere you boarded?"

Harrowby, near at hand, laughed aloud at that. After a moment, so did Captain Utterson.

"I'll not begrudge you that saying," he vowed. "For us, we were outgunned and trapped with scant room to fight in. A mast was down on us, and never in these thirty years at sea have I been in worse case. No doubt but that we'd have been sunk or captured but for you. But what I meant was, you're no King's men. Just what are you, then?"

"I fear we're what you'd call pirates, sir," replied Haws. "Outlaws and exiles and rovers of the sea. And you yourself have just done us the kindness to say, we were your salvation."

"Pirates or devils, our debt to you is great," agreed Utterson, nodding his hard face. "I say it's high time for you and me to have a talk." He gestured. "Come aboard the *Jason,* sir. You and your officers. We'll sit together in my cabin—"

"By your leave, Captain Utterson," interrupted Haws, wiping the blade of his sword. "Any sane pirate must pause before coming aboard a King's ship. Consultation there might find him at a disadvantage."

"I take your meaning, " Utterson smiled. "Well, I have no such hesitation. I'll go talk with you in your own cabin."

Haws slid his sword carefully into its sheath. "Alack," he said, "I gave my Doctor leave to use our cabins as hospital space for those of our crew who were wounded."

Utterson beckoned a young officer. "Lieutenant, have you inspected the Captain's quarters aboard this captured ship?"

"That have I, sir," replied the other, saluting. "They're splendid quarters, too."

"Then suppose you conduct us thither," Utterson told him. "Come along, sir—Captain Haws, you call yourself. And if you like, fetch this young man who took the Spaniard's sword in battle."

Haws beckoned Ranald. They went aft together, and down a flight of steps. Captain Utterson opened a door, and they went into a spacious compartment. It was more luxuriously furnished than any cabin aboard any ship Ranald had ever visited. It was nothing like what he imagined in a ship of war. The dark woodwork was bordered with gold leaf, the furniture showed intricate, rich carving, and hangings and tablecloth were of embroidered silk. The British Lieutenant dragged the curtains from two square ports to give them light.

Utterson opened a cabinet and rummaged inside. "Ah," he said with deep satisfaction, "here's a bottle of Spanish wine, and 'twill be first-class, I'll warrant you. On the rack yonder I see silver goblets."

Ranald fetched four of the goblets and set them at the table. Utterson uncorked the bottle and filled the goblets. They all sat at the table, and Utterson bracketed his chin in his hand and gazed searchingly at Haws.

"So you call yourself a pirate, eh?" he said at last.

"What I said was, that you would call me a pirate," Haws reminded him.

Again Utterson flashed his smile. "Sir, I have four interesting things to tell you," he announced. "The first of these I have more or less said already. I credit you and your ship and your men with saving me and the *Jason* and all aboard her from death or capture at Spanish hands. You will not, as I predict, find me ungrateful."

"That's very kindly said, sir," Haws remarked.

"And honestly said, too," Utterson assured him. "But here's to our better acquaintance."

He lifted his goblet. They all drank. Utterson shifted his gaze to Ranald.

"I've not yet had the pleasure of hearing this young gentleman's name," he said.

"Ranald Blaikie, our Quartermaster," Haws said. "Aboard our rover ships, Captain Utterson, the Quartermaster is an important officer."

"I see, I see," muttered the English Captain, nodding to Ranald, then at Haws. "Well, sir, we come to the second thing I have to tell you. Or have you already guessed it?"

"Guessed it, sir?" echoed Haws. "Not I."

"Ha!" Utterson snapped out a laugh. "I take leave to say, you have a very good notion of what it is. For you and I have known each other in the past. As sure as my name is Warrick Utterson, your name is not Reuben Haws, but Joseph Shaw, who fled from England a quarter of a century gone as an accused rebel."

# safe return ⚓16⚓

Shocked silence then. Ranald saw Haws grow pale. The young Lieutenant's eyes grew large. Ranald stared. Only Captain Warrick Utterson seemed at ease. He smiled again, but gently this time.

"Surely you didn't think I would mistake you," he said to Haws. "You knew me on sight. Of that I felt sure."

Haws shrugged his shoulders, as though in defeat.

"Yes, I knew you," he admitted. "A quarter of a century has passed, but we were too close friends back then to forget each other. It's as you say. I was out in 1715 for James Stuart, to help put him on the throne in place of George the First. But James Stuart had to flee to save himself, and so did I. I've been fleeing ever since."

Ranald had heard of that rebellion that had come to nothing before he was born. His father had talked of James and his claim to the British crown, and of how some had rallied to his cause. It had come to nothing, as Ranald remembered the story.

"You were young then, no older than Mr. Blaikie here," said Utterson. "Your good old father was sore hurt by what you did, Joseph."

"My father," said Haws. "Is he—"

"Alive and hearty in his old age, when last I saw him," said Utterson. "You'll recollect, I knew him well. I was in his shipping business, already an officer aboard one of his ships out of Dundee, and I had his friendship and confidence. He and I both grieved sorely for you."

Haws shrugged again. "I fled, and I was lucky I could do so. Others on the side of James Stuart were hanged for their action."

"I can remember several," said Utterson. "That was long ago, however, and excitement and vengefulness have died down at home."

"But I became a gentleman of fortune," Haws reminded. "A sea rover. What you call a pirate."

"That fetches us to the third thing I will tell you," said Utterson, pouring more wine for himself. "And it partakes somewhat of the first thing. I am Captain of the frigate *Jason,* twenty-four guns, and she will sail and fight again as quickly as we can rig that foremast the Spaniards shot away from us. And not a man aboard her but will say with me, if harm or blame is offered you, 'twill never befall you save over our dead bodies."

"You are kind, Warrick," said Haws again. "Perhaps the fourth thing you have to tell me is that the *Tuscarora,* with all her crew, may depart in peace."

Utterson shook his bandaged head violently. "Never that, sir. I will insist that you come with the *Jason* and this captured *Compeador* to Edenton."

Ranald thought of the Edenton jail from which he and Pilbeam had escaped. Could he hope to escape again?

"To Edenton you shall come, and every man of your crew," said Utterson, emphasizing every word. "Do not frown as though I am not sensible of my debt to you. Because we come to that fourth matter."

He sipped wine, while they all watched him silently.

"Reflect, Joseph," he said, "that George the First hath been at rest these dozen years and more. His son, our second George, is compassionate from time to time. Through the years, he hath found himself able to pardon a number of those rebels, who never really were able to harm his father. And of late, your father and his friends—myself among them—have been able to offer your name to him as one who may have been reckless in youth but never a criminal."

"Sir, I don't take your meaning," said Haws.

"Then suffer me to make it clear. One day, after a good dinner, King George was pleased to sign a proclamation which said that, wherever you had vanished, you were free to come home, to live in peace and safety."

Haws half started from his chair. "Warrick, you jest!" he cried.

"Would I jest of such matters? Believe me, Joseph, for I have seen the document. As for your being a pirate—why, there's a wise, useful policy these days of granting amnesty to such folk, if they'll come in and swear loyalty.

For, as we have seen but now, pirates are the best of sea-fighters. If they turn honest, they'll be of precious service in this war with Spain."

All this Captain Utterson had said in the calmest and friendliest of ways, while watching Haws closely. Now he turned his attention to Ranald.

"By heaven, your young Quartermaster hears all these things in greater amazement than you," he remarked. "His eyes start forth like a crab's. What say you, Quartermaster Blaikie? Will you help me talk over my old friend Joseph Shaw to return and serve his King, or would you rather range and raid and ravage as a pirate?"

"Sir, I but seek to comprehend all this great good fortune," Ranald stammered out. "I've been of this pirate company, true enough, but that was a sorry trick of fate. Ask Captain Haws to tell you—"

"Call me Joseph Shaw," said Haws. "That is my rightful name, though I've not used it these many years. Blaikie is right, Warrick. He was more or less impressed aboard, and made to sign our articles. But he hath kept his honor. All in our company admire him for that. As for piracy, never did he help take a ship except two Spanish merchants."

"You forget the *Compeador*," Utterson reminded him, smiling. "Spanish she may be, but no merchant save of destruction. Zounds, gentlemen, she's as rich a prize as could be taken, and all who helped in the taking may look for a share of the profits at the hands of the government."

Haws got to his feet. "I'll go assemble my crew," he

said. "When they hear your fair offer, I predict they'll all gladly take their pardons and do their duty for the King."

"Lieutenant Blythe," Utterson addressed his subordinate, "I'll put you in command of a prize crew aboard the *Compeador,* to fetch her to Edenton. And mayhap Captain Shaw will lend you Quartermaster Blaikie, to steer you through these Carolina waters."

They had been ashore at Edenton for five days.

The *Tuscarora,* the *Jason* and the *Compeador* were anchored in Albemarle Sound, just clear of the docks. Townspeople gaped and wondered at that great captured ship, its red sides pocked and splintered by cannon balls, and they told the tale of how her coffers had yielded up forty thousand pieces of eight, to be divided among the men who took her. They gaped, too, at the Spanish prisoners in a waterside warehouse, under the guard of self-important militiamen. Still more excitedly they gaped at the gay-shirted, grinning pirates who lounged on the streets and in the taverns, seemingly as welcome in Edenton as the British sailors and marines.

Governor Gabriel Johnston held a meeting in the office at the rear of his mansion, with seven men he had summoned there. Captain Utterson and Lieutenant Blythe sat in chairs opposite the Governor's desk, clad in their most splendid uniforms. On a settee were seated Joseph Shaw, no longer Reuben Haws, and Dr. Pilbeam, also in their frilled and gold-buttoned best. Captain Mandeville, just back from his voyage to England, was there, along with his partner Mr. Blaikie who had hurried up from

Bath at the Governor's call. And by a rear window Ranald watched a little group of ladies among the flowers—the Governor's stately wife, Mrs. Blaikie and Mrs. Mandeville, and tall, dark Enid.

Governor Johnston dipped a quill pen in ink and signed his name to a document, then to another document, then to another. He was a man of forty-two, with a high-boned, rosy face and brown hair. As he finished with each, he put it on a stack of sheets at his elbow. At last he laid down the quill and looked around at his companions.

"That's the lot, sirs," he announced. "Some forty times have I written out my name, to pardon all your company, Captain Shaw. Aye, every man of them, as they appear on your ship's articles. Upon my soul, 'tis a happy labor with me to do so."

"I venture to trust, Your Excellency, that you took note of my special case," said Dr. Pilbeam.

"I did that, Doctor, and with the utmost of pleasure. That ancient charge of traitorous outlawry seems far less odious when carefully studied. It now goes for naught."

"And the same for Ranald Blaikie?" Pilbeam suggested.

The Governor turned his eyes toward Ranald, who still stared out the window.

"Oh, there's no pardon for young Mr. Blaikie," said Governor Johnston. "Just a note, somewhat in the nature of an apology for the hasty, rough use and menace he encountered here, when he was undeserving of either."

Captain Mandeville grinned toward Ranald's inattentive back. "There remains the matter of the *Tuscarora*, the property of myself and my partner Mr. Blaikie of Bath," he said. "As Your Excellency knows, we have spoken with Captain Shaw. With your approval, we are ready to send our ship out as a privateer. Thus we can be of service to our colony."

"Aye, and you may look for owners' shares in the value of enemy ships taken," added Utterson.

"That will be swiftly accomplished," Johnston promised. "I will issue you letters of marque. You, Captain Shaw, will want to sail promptly."

"At once, if it please Your Excellency," Shaw assured him. "With that good ship, and the men who sail her . . ."

"Wait, old friend," broke in Utterson. "See to my case. We wait for commission from home, to refit and put to sea with that captured warship *Compeador*. I may reasonably expect to command her, having fetched her in; and Blythe here looks as hopefully to command the *Jason*. But we both need men of pluck, and I bespeak a share of yours, as soon as they are sworn into service."

Shaw smiled. "I must leave that decision to the men, Warrick. Let them choose with whom they'll sail and fight."

"Then I'll begin by asking your young Quartermaster," said Utterson. "What then, young sir, will you ship with me? Ranald Blaikie, I speak to you."

Ranald turned from the window. "I pray your pardon, sir?"

"I want you as an officer upon the *Compeador* when

we sail out after Spaniards," said Utterson. "How say you to being Second Mate?"

"Stop ere you reply to him," said Shaw quickly. "These King's ships must wait long weeks for word from London. But the *Tuscarora* is ready to go privateering. Why not be First Mate aboard her, with me and Harrowby and Terrell and all the others you know?"

"Gentlemen," stammered Ranald, "I—I—Your Excellency, if Captain Shaw will have me with the *Tuscarora,* I am happy to go."

"Come, gentlemen, we've decided the chief points of our business," said the Governor then. "Shall we join the ladies out yonder?"